STORM

STORM

MINDS SHINE BRIGHT
SEASONS 1 2023

Editor: Amanda Scotney
writing@mindsshinebright.com

Published by Minds Shine Bright in 2023
PO Box 1042
Windsor, 3181, VIC, Australia
Website: www.mindsshinebright.com
Subscribe: www.mindsshinebright.com/minds-shine-bright-blog
Twitter: @msbwriting
Facebook: Minds Shine Bright|Melbourne VIC
Copyediting by Words Worthwhile
Proofreading by Millie Shilland
Book design and layout by Ampersand Duck
Cover artwork by Mike Barr, *Weather at the Museum*, 2020, acrylic on canvas
www.bluethumb.com.au/mike-barr/
Printed by IngramSpark

ISBN 978-0-6455231-2-6

A catalogue record for this
book is available from the
National Library of Australia

Minds Shine Bright acknowledges the people of the Kulin Nation, the Traditional
Custodians of the land on which we live and work and where we have created
this anthology. We pay respects to their long history and culture, and their
Elders past and present.

Special thanks to my friends and family who have supported and encouraged
me behind the scenes; and to the libraries, schools, and arts and writers'
organisations that have helped writing and reading to flourish in safe havens;
and to all those who have helped to promote the Minds Shine Bright writing
competitions and anthologies. Thanks to all writers, poets and screenwriters
who have submitted their work to Minds Shine Bright.

This publication includes strong themes, images and language. Parental
guidance is recommended for younger readers.

Aboriginal and Torres Strait Islander readers are advised that this book contains
an image of a deceased person.

CONTENTS

INTRODUCTION

AMANDA SCOTNEY

There is something about storms that brings out the primal in us; a mixture of wonder and awe, and the best and the worst of human nature. *Storm* is the first anthology in the *Seasons* series by Minds Shine Bright that explores themes relating to the external environment.

This collection of short stories, poetry and flash fiction featuring the winning and commended entries from the Minds Shine Bright Storm writing competition provides something new for lovers of storm writing.

Storm will move you, delight you and make you think. Join the Minds Shine Bright writers and poets on a journey to stormy places, discover people and animals along the way, and explore different worlds and possible futures.

Minds Shine Bright is an arts business based in Melbourne, Australia, that runs two writing competitions each year and publishes books. Our aim is to raise the profiles of our writers and to ensure that every published writer receives payment in the form of prize money. In the longer term, we aim to build a business model that enables ongoing payment of royalties to our writers and poets. This will take time, consistent effort and ongoing collaboration to promote the magic of anthologies to new audiences and build a wider readership.

In addition to our *Seasons* series and competitions, we also run an annual competition, Minds Shine Bright *Confidence*, which explores the theme of confidence in fiction, poetry and scripts. If you love *Storm*, you might like to explore our *Confidence* series too. You can purchase Minds Shine Bright anthologies in print and e-book format at www.mindsshinebright.com/shop and at many good bookshops.

Over the last year, when *Storm* entries were being written, there were a series of extreme weather events across the globe. The United States was hit hard by weather events; in Europe, there was drought as well as fires, flooding and earthquakes; in Asia, there were floods in Afghanistan, India, Bangladesh, Pakistan and Thailand, drought in China and some Pacific Island nations, and typhoons in the Philippines; and in eastern Australia, there was much rain and flooding too.

This affected some of the Minds Shine Bright writers at the *Confidence Minds Shine Bright Anthology 2022* launch last year, when writers from regional

Victoria travelled along flood-impacted roads to attend the event at the Wheeler Centre in Melbourne.

ENTRANTS' INTERPRETATIONS OF THE STORM THEME

There were almost four hundred entries to the *Storm* writing competition, from Australia, the United States, Europe and Asia. Entrants ranged in age from under twelve to over eighty. Two primary schools entered groups of students. The following analysis is across all submitted entries.

A rage of writing approaches emerged, including visual feasts of storm-scapes, stormy struggles and characters, and pieces that make you think about the fundamental nature of things – what it is to be human and what may lie ahead for us all.

THE HERO'S JOURNEY

The role of the hero, as they struggled through the storm, was to keep others safe. The hero would put other people or animals before their own comfort or safety, and they sometimes sacrificed their own life to save others. Some examples of heroes included lighthouse keepers, seafarers, and a boy who was left alone to care for all the animals in a deserted house. Characters travelled to find adventure and love, or to build new lives.

INNER TURMOIL

There were many storms that brewed and swirled inside the minds of characters. From something as simple as writer's block to grief, anger, and despair. Many of the storms related to mental health issues, and others were linked to the impacts of alcohol and drugs on people and communities. The impacts of domestic violence, and the physical and emotional damage it inflicts, were explored too. Whilst inner turmoil was a serious subject matter, some writing had a lyrical beauty about it, particularly where there was also a connection with nature.

THE CLAY

Life moulds and changes us like a potter working with clay. For some characters, war was the storm they endured, and this had a significant impact on their lives and choices. A father was seen in a new way as he sat with his daughter during a hurricane. The wisdom of older hands helped to read the oncoming storms.

THE DANCE OF LIFE

Heavy rain and impending storms set a wonderful contrast to the vivacity of life and longing. Two people made love in the sticky heat, with a storm approaching. A woman contemplated the shift from being a young person out on the town to the reality of being a sleep-poor parent. An old woman set the morning fire.

THE PURPLE FANTASTIC

Fantasy writing featured imaginary worlds, castles, battles, science fiction, future climate stress, magic and magical powers, time travel and historical fiction. Beachcombers collected body parts to tend to war-injured Andalonians and Firkkners, and a man struck by lightning "travelled" through time as he wandered the streets of Melbourne at night.

The darkest storm writing was about death, dying and the end of the world. The light went out forever when the laptop battery lost its charge.

STORMY PLACES, PEOPLE AND ANIMALS

Some writing sought to harness the immense power of water. During storms, people and shelters were exposed, fragile and insubstantial compared to the power of nature. These interpretations remind us that everything we have, including our lives, could be swept away and destroyed in a moment, before the sun comes out to shine again.

Like photographs, some pieces captured the elemental beauty of storms from particular places such as Ketchum Bay, Newtown Bridge, and Lake Alexandrina.

There were some beautiful stories and poems written about animals in storms: the sad spirit who could not find where he belonged until he was reunited with the spirits of his extinct kind; the gryphon who learned to fly in a storm; a pack of wolves observed on a cold winter's night; and the storm-like qualities of an animal's eyes.

The stories of people in the landscape and in storms often needed few words to express much meaning. There were a range of stormy characters too who stumbled through life, caused chaos and entertained.

Impending storms brought out stresses and awkwardness in family dynamics, allowing family members to see each other in a new way and giving some people the courage to make changes.

RURAL AND URBAN

Rural storms usually occurred outdoors on a farm or in a natural setting, whereas urban storms tended to be experienced or viewed from inside, looking out. There were many references to teacups and storms in teacups. Teacups were used as a symbol of camaraderie, calmness, and the cosmos and all that it contains. Broken teacups or mugs symbolised discord or violence.

THE PHILOSOPHY OF STORMS

Some of the more philosophical writing in *Storm* inspired reflection about core values and responsibilities. In particular, the storm of war raised some interesting philosophical questions: What if your home was destroyed by a war and you had to find shelter? What kind of person would you choose to be – the kind that makes war or the kind that helps others get back up when they are down?

The fragility and the privilege of shelter raised other questions. We have shelter and are privileged to have it, but we are part of the bigger natural world too. Where does our responsibility start and how far should it go?

My mind is filled with images of the misty wetness of eucalypts and the squawking of parrots as they rise and flock before oncoming rain. This is partly from reading *Storm* entries, mixed with memories of my recent trip through the Blue Mountains to Mudgee, and partly from the chattering birds outside and the low-hanging rain clouds beyond.

This anthology forms part of the long history of storytelling, songs and poetry about storms. As you read, you will glimpse the hugeness of storms, how they influence characters, animals and landscapes, and how we as humans interpret and connect with the elements. *Storm* is the first anthology in the Minds Shine Bright *Seasons* series that explores external environments. Curating *Storm* has been a joyful and inspirational experience, and I hope you enjoy your reading journey as much as I did.

1

TOP TEN

FIRST PRIZE

DR CHELINAY GATES
GUILDFORD, WA, AUSTRALIA

Dr Chelinay Gates (aka Malardy Malardy) is an Indigenous artist, author, playwright, poet and Doctor of Traditional Chinese Medicine. She finds writing is an important way to distil the meaning of life by sharing its stories.

STORM CLOUDS APPROACHING

Outside, it's still dark . . .

A white-haired old woman coughs as she stirs from under a pile of old blankets. She and her old dog sleep on a tatty old mattress on the ground outside a tiny tin hut. Her left hand rummages under the corner of her mattress, looking for a box of matches. She struggles to her feet and stretches out her old body, leaving her dog curled up in the blankets. She pops the matches into the pocket of her long skirt . . . it's new. Softly, she sings a greeting to Country and the Great Spirits, all the while, her hands keep a constant rhythm, dancing silently in the air.

Then humming quietly, she shuffles her feet in the sand while collecting twigs and pieces of cardboard from last night's discarded flagons. The campfire's gone out . . . Storm clouds are approaching. Rubbing her cold hands together, she blows her warm breath into them, then pauses for a moment to look around. Squatting down, she arranges the bits of cardboard and twigs. Reaching into her pocket she takes a fire stick out of the box and strikes it, lighting up the little pile she's made.

The Morning Star is greeted by the chirp of crickets and little birds waking. Carolling magpies announce the dawn. Streaks of lavender and pink leak out above the horizon, but the Sun, She hesitates, just below a heavy line of blue-grey clouds . . . waiting for the perfect moment to reveal herself and her golden entourage.

The old girl gathers some gum tree and wattle branches and places them on the crackling fire. A sweet plume of smoke uncoils like a snake as it rises high into the dawning sky. Sitting by the fire, she takes a deep breath and sings softly in her mother tongue.

Elfie, her granddaughter, is freezing. She runs out of the old tin hut, wrapped in a torn blanket. Leaving the door open, she plops down and snuggles her ear into Aunty Hazel's chest . . . listening to that ancient song that echoes in Aunty's breast.

From the tiny tin hut, Elfie's mum's high-pitched voice sings out . . .

"Aun-ee Hazel! . . . Love a cuppa!"

Elfie

Aunty Hazel

SECOND PRIZE

CASSIE BOULIS
ATLANTA, GEORGIA, UNITED STATES

Cassie Boulis is an eighteen-year-old writer living in Atlanta, Georgia. Through her writing, she explores themes of adolescence, the LGBTQ+ experience and familial relationships. She has had her art and writing featured in Beyond Words *and* Artwife *literary magazines and has had seventeen recognitions from the Scholastic Art & Writing Awards.*

THE THAW

My father's skin hangs off him like the rind of a grapefruit. Every time I hug him, it feels as if I have carried the weight of his skin, and I remember my mother's words: you will never understand someone's life until you have chosen to walk in their shoes.

Silently, I observe my father as he completes his work, contemplating him over the milk cartons. Maybe age is just the separation of a soul from a body. I am hoping, for his sake, that the pock marks on his arms are the exit wounds.

Time is a knife, and it has carved him.

His hands are gnarled, as if he has been shrinking from the inside and has felt the weight of his body caving in.

I am realizing that I have never seen my father before. I have looked at him from across the breakfast table. I have heard him in the copper door hinges at 2 am, in the rush of water in the sink, in the shower. I have seen him, but I've never looked at him before.

The cigarette between my father's teeth flares. Outside, the powerlines crack like whips as they unwind. They are black coiled snakes surging over the tiles of the roof. Their cotton mouths are full of stars. Between me and him, the milk cartons begin to tremble, and we sit there quiet as our power goes out. The sound of the broken television is like many conversations I have had with my father – it is a lost connection.

We sit in the darkness for an instant, and by the time the cigarette has faded, the entire room is black.

"Your mother would have liked this, you know?" he tells me. "She liked it when it rained best."

Like sparks, his voice intensifies and then fades to black, and I think it is the only form of electricity left in our house.

Florida is too cold tonight, and the hurricane is approaching, and our love is seventeen years behind us, but here I am, with him, in the kitchen, watching the milk cartons titter.

I want to reach my father, but there is a hurricane between us.

"She wouldn't have let the milk spoil," I tell him.

In the darkness, the radioman tells us a secret. It will be at least two hours before our power is back on. The secret is that the entire city has gone dark. The secret is that the next time we will see light is when the sun rises, egg yolks dripping through our windowsills.

The television shreds itself with static.

The radioman warns us that a storm is approaching. He tells us to cover our windows, to lock ourselves away from the outside. He tells us not to open the windows, to leave the doors locked.

When he is silent, there is no wind, and

It is quiet again between us.

I find myself asking that the hurricane comes soon and quickly and completely, and I hope it consumes the space between us and leaves no silence.

Sometimes, the only weapon I have is my own voice, and so

I am humming a song, and it is a silent prayer.

O Mother, if you can hear me, take me back to when I was too young to know that anything could scar

me permanently. Come back to me.

"Before you got old, I used to play you songs before bed."

I notice that I cannot see his teeth as he talks. His breath pushes through him like the blue neon of an X-ray.

Outside, the trees split, playing us a tune on the dirt.

As bad as the weather is, the wind feels as constant as a sideways gravity. The shadows of strangers are like blades of licorice, black as the hour.

"I remember," I say. "Before your fingers started going numb."

The refrigerator is almost empty. All that's left between us are a couple of coolers of ice and the big gray machine.

"I was hoping you would play something for me."

"I don't know how to," I say. What I do not say is that I want to believe in new beginnings, but if that were true, then why is it that the clock never starts at zero.

He takes up an oak guitar, running his hands over its neck as if it is ana-tomy. He touches it as tenderly as if it were his wife.

"That's all right. I remember." The wind pushes between us and knocks on the windows, a reminder of the ghost among us.

Sometimes, I hear the wind, and I do not know if God is a season or if my mother has come home. She knocks on the picture frames.

In his numb hands, he releases notes, and they fly away, lost birds through empty windows. Beside us, the milk cartons dance but do not spill. I watch him struggle, pressing the strings into the pads of his fingers until they turn his palms pink.

He's angry that he cannot feel them through the layers of his skin, and I realize that

Time is a knife that he has not felt.

"Dad. Let me try." I take the guitar from him and play a few cold notes which intensify, and

My body is an echo, and so I speak for him.

He puts his hands on top of my own, and I am just now realizing that

Your body is the language that your soul speaks.

We strum.

It is a collective voice.

Beside me, the empty fridge has swung open, cooling us down from the inside.

Outside, the wind pushes houses over as if they were aspens in a drought.

Inside, everything around us is thawing.

THIRD PRIZE

TROY WALSH

WYANGALA, NSW, AUSTRALIA

Troy Walsh lives on Wiradjuri country in Central West NSW. He is forty-something and has previously masqueraded as an outdoor guide, rural journalist and garlic farmer.

IN THE EMBRACE OF TREES

Leaves flickering. What was just a few soft sounds, slow, deliberate, hidden, suddenly became a disturbance in the canopy. Caught in the light of a just-waning moon, the unfamiliar movement dragged on the owl's attention. From its loftier perch in an old gum tree, the owl left its pondering of the rough cover of grass that lay in the space between the occupied tree and the wooden slats of the nearby house's back fence.

The moon had risen to a position of midday's summer sun; part of somewhere else's daylight reflecting across the pale, dead lawn. Shadows sharply contrasted under the clothesline.

No scurry of mice, slither of serpent or beast of bug crossed within the owl's watch.

Distracted. Falling, swooping, the owl arrived for a closer look. It sat on the highest pitch of the roof. The owl did not expect to see the boy in the tree.

Whether the boy held the tree or the tree held the boy in its heights, the owl did not immediately discern. In the dappled light, the boy's bare arms intertwined with the branches. Perched, facing outwards, the boy's bare trunk nestled against the bough of the tree. His legs extended out of a pair of pyjama shorts. One fell across and dangled over the larger branch he sat on while the other leg, bent, rested against a smaller branch.

When I was younger, my parents would tell the story about me sleepwalking – or more aptly, sleep climbing – in a tree outside our early childhood home.

I was a fervent arbour adventurer by day, but I don't remember this incident.

It was always a good interjection for my mother – when the conversation turned to what to do with such a wanderer-of-the-night. She would say, "We left him be, and eventually he made his own way down", or thereabouts.

I do remember sleepwalking a couple of other times, though, when my mother or father didn't find me or even know to be looking in those resting hours: once I stood, facing the side of the house, confused. The dark, thick bushes blocking the way to the front of the house and the street; and another time pissing in a derelict garden bed.

Maybe I was even a strange-sort-of-proud at the mention of my nocturnal escapades.

I don't think my parents gave it too much thought really.

Similarly, they showed no concern about all the hours and days spent roaming the edge of our rural town, where I lived during those primary school years. Bands of boys, occasionally a sister, poked and pushed the boundaries of our world, mostly without too much hassle.

I don't remember a name for the type of tree that grew outside the backdoor of my family's small, ramshackle, brick home with its add-on room out back and the toilet further afield. The faded, peeling white paint contrasting with the tree's glossy, lush-green, elliptical leaves and small blackberries.

I can recall that it grew with a child in mind. There were enough branches, not too rough, that were strong and formed into handy climbing shapes. I attempted a cubby house in its branches.

A couple of years later, my father's fortunes rode a horse all the way to the bank. Or more directly, to building a new home for us on a block next door.

It wasn't my tree anymore. I did help finish something grander and sinister in its branches though.

Together with the new, older-boy owner of the tree, we created a fortress to plan and launch nightly, paint-bomb-style attacks on an old friend/new enemy a few houses around the corner. In the aftermath, my dad, me, and my apologetic words, met with another dad on our new verandah.

The tree I recollect more vividly was a large river red gum up the road. Away from the bank's edge, the eucalypt was straighter, the lower branches high, further apart. Its towering size was a standing challenge in the neighbourhood. My brother and the older boys he rode around with would drop their bikes and climb, executing daring moves, possum-like, into its expanse.

The trouble for us youngsters was a leap from one of the lower branches to grab one higher up. The fall was from a nasty height onto a mess of peeling bark, burls, uneven roots and hard ground.

Making it to the branch for the leap was the first test. But that climb only qualified that you might not be big enough to even attempt it. I do remember the fear, that rising ebb of adrenaline, heavy with dread, that I wasn't going to land my hands on that pale, smooth, muscular, yellow arm sticking out. I didn't, couldn't, let it linger long. I knew that someone else had done it, and so I barely jumped into glory. Higher up, any of the older boys who had bothered to watch were left disappointed.

Getting down was just as, or more, difficult and scary. It wasn't something I repeated often before asphalt and more houses came along and the old red gum sentinel disappeared.

In my mid-twenties, it happened that I didn't hit the branch that well. I ended up with a busted ankle and hours of crawling, hopping and the popping of pain. Two young ladies were there to observe my decision to make an impromptu Tarzan leap to an outstretched limb while bushwalking off a peak named Mount Amos. All both the women could do was stare at me dumb-faced through my extended struggle down the mountain side and back to the car.

My failure to get a good swing on the branch that day and make it clearly over the boulder below blew more than any romantic chances I was seeding. The executives running the eco-style resort on the east coast of Tasmania, where I was building my outdoor-guiding career, were obliged to cancel my management training scheduled for the next day.

A couple of years later, I would make another leap, where failure meant crunching into rock. I was coming down a big dangerous granite face, once again on dire slopes of The Hazards. Made it that day. Dropping, swooping, hitting, swinging, landing. No audience.

As for sleepwalking, it doubled back on me under the guise of alcohol blackouts. Binge-drinking damage. The constant lurching off into the dark when the drinks were flowing.

Ridiculous exploits, extreme banality, explosions or disappearances at all hours, even when alone. The abyss I stepped into was not always the same. Sometimes there was somebody watching. Sometimes the consequences were the only answers, and the questions were lost permanently.

The worst moments in my life have come to me while standing and trying to figure out how the hard, reformed, reality that now faced me differed from the one I left half-pissed hours earlier.

I find myself sitting on the banks of Kalari's bustling brown water. Under a river red gum, gnarled and magnificent in its existence, a point of resistance to the centuries that have passed by it. I find myself here, not really anywhere. I am hidden from the outside world. The teenage girls on the opposite bank are also seeking concealment, to spark up a smoke.

My thirst is as rapid as the flow below my feet, the low-sugar, blue cider cans drop to the grass.

Walking along a dark highway into blackness. Large trees by the side of the road, an avenue through time and space. River red gums, with wide-spreading heights and broad, gnarled bases, stand among whispering she-oaks. The drought-hardy pepper trees planted a century or more ago, rivals in the landscape.

A rumbling sound coming. Stalking a dangerous beast. Blinding lights, the honking of a horn, a truck. A rush of wind and then calm. For a few moments, the night breathes deep and slowly.

A glimpse in the darkness, a slim point of orientation.

A head-on with the world coming up around the bend.

Thunder from Tartarus, chaos and havoc. A storm rages up on the flood plain. Witnesses. Emergency services.

What did the owl see?

The conversation never sidetracks to sleepwalking anymore. What to do with the wanderer-of-the-night is no longer an opportunity for my mother to interject. No answer is wanted or ever was. The details are forgotten, and what barely remains, has been obscured over time. Connections have been lost; branches have fallen.

My parents and I no longer are.

FOURTH PRIZE

SARAH RASMUSSEN
KORUMBURRA, VIC, AUSTRALIA

Sarah Rasmussen is a writer and reviewer based in South Gippsland, Victoria. She created the blog Ragamuffin Books, *where she writes about children's and young adult fiction. She also reviews books for* Kids' Book Reviews. *She has recently finished her Master's degree in writing and is currently working on a number of projects.*

HOUSE OF FEATHERS

There is a home here, somewhere, under all of these lost things. There was a family that once lived here. But now, there are claws and beaks and skittering. There are teeth and fruit and flies. There is dung and fur and feathers.

But there is also a boy.

He is mostly made of feathers – skinny, shrunken limbs; black, downy hair; and dark beetle eyes. He has no bed but sleeps on the couch. He wears the same clothes almost every day – a faded red T-shirt and once-blue footy shorts. He wakes early, on the eve of dawn. He searches the house for food, but there is only feed for the animals – seeds and nuts. He eats them anyway. Then he goes about his chores.

He whistles as he walks along the dirt-covered floorboards to one of the bedrooms, where the birds live. He opens the door and pours some seed on the ground, then steps back from the screeching – the cloud of greens and blues and reds. There are parakeets and lorikeets and rosellas and galahs and quails and fairy-wrens.

There is also one cockatoo.

"Good morning!" a tinny voice says.

The boy smiles and replies, "Good morning, Ted."

Ted's golden crest unfolds as he batters his big white wings before taking flight and perching on the boy's shoulder. He will stay with him all day. The door snaps shut behind them, and the boy walks to the other bedroom, with nuts and leaves in his dirty hands.

He carefully creaks the door open and sits cross-legged in the middle of the second bedroom and closes his eyes. This room consists of huge tree branches, so tall they only fit in diagonally and stretch from the ground up to the high ceilings.

The sound of small scurrying feet reaches the boy's ears, so he holds out his hand, gentle and welcoming. The soft nose of the bravest tickles his palm, and he sneaks a glance from under his lashes to see the big male's shiny black eyes. Next, the sugar glider lands at his feet and hops into the food. Then the rest come – the brutal brush-tails and the fragile ringtail possums. He sees the mamma ringtail, with her baby clinging to her back. She never approaches him since she had her joey, so the boy steps out of the room to leave them to themselves.

He heads outside and feeds the rest of the animals. The dogs all tail along behind him – kelpies and heelers and Pomeranians.

Eventually, after they are fed, he sits in the sunshine on the back deck amongst the wreckage, just him and Ted. He eats a few more sunflower seeds from his pocket and watches the animals scatter around the large backyard. It is a forest out here, and the grass grows wild, hiding old trampolines, pieces of metal and memories. Ted jumps down from his shoulder and hops along the deck, the clacking of his claws vibrates through the old timber.

"Beautiful day!" Ted screeches.

"Sure is, Ted."

The sun streams through the eucalyptus trees, and the morning mist still clings to the air. It is a little cold though, but the dogs don't feel it, so neither does he.

The biggest kelpie lets out a mighty woof, and the boy's ears prick up.

"They are here. They are here!" Ted squawks.

The crunch of tyres on gravel meets his ears, and the boy scatters to the edge of the deck and peeks around the house. He sees blues and reds. A man and a woman sit in the front seat of the car, with bored but wary looks on their faces. The boy freezes for a while, a possum stuck in the middle of the road. The slam of the car door brings him out of his stupor, and he steps back and scuttles up the poles to the roof. He inches his way along the tiles, careful not to let any slip.

A firm knock resounds through the house, and the boy hears the animal response, the chirps and scrapes.

"Open up. Victoria Police."

He hopes they will go away and leave him be, but they don't. He hears one of the windows slide open, and a thump from below tells him the policeman is inside. The creak of the unused front door soon follows. It prickles him to know they are here, in his haven. Fear spreads through his limbs like boiling water.

He runs.

He flies off the roof, as graceful as a glider, and makes for the trees in the backyard, scampering and climbing until he can get as high as possible. The dogs bark and try to chase him, but he shoos them away, and they listen. Ted's claws dig into his shoulder as he climbs, but he is glad for the company. The boy clings to the trunk of the gum tree and waits, watching the old, white weatherboard house. From above, he can see how run-down it is – the peeling paint and rotten windows. Half the deck is missing from the wrap-around verandah. But it is still home to him.

After a while, he hears the car start up and drive along the street. He climbs down and makes his way back to the house, tail between his legs.

The house is the same, except the animals are all hushed, afraid. The presence of someone unknown trails through the house. The boy checks every room, every animal. He goes to the possum room and sits on the floor.

Tears form in his eyes, and his hands shake. He knows the police will return; they are like wolves – they hunt in packs. They will return with more people, other people. They will take him and stick him somewhere else – somewhere clean and white and empty. There will be no more animals, no soft fur and non-judgemental eyes. He will be put in a home with a family that doesn't care for him, and they will take his family and put them in cages, not knowing that this is their home, just like it is his. Why can't they just let him be?

He does his afternoon chores, but there is sadness in his movements. He no longer whistles, or dances between the rooms. His mind is full.

A decision must be made.

His first instinct is to run – to gather food and leave it in big bags all over the house for the animals. They would survive. But maybe they would turn feral and eat each other, tear the skin and meat from each other's bones. And how would he get them the food? It's hard enough to sustain them now, let alone in big piles.

He disregards the thought, as he could never abandon them. That would make him just like her.

Then perhaps he would have to set them all free. Open the windows and watch them fly. He could run with them, follow them to wherever they go. Gallop alongside the dogs, leap through the trees after the possums, or follow the shadows of the birds to a great forest. He would learn to hunt and live peacefully, away from the mess of humans. This idea is the most appealing so far, and he likes to live in it for a while.

But as the day passes, he knows that it won't happen. That he could never coax all the animals out, that they would just be caught and put in cages. They are not made for the true wild, and neither is he.

This leaves him only one option. He must fight, for a storm is coming.

It starts to rain as he begins his preparations.

It is daylight again by the time he is finished, though no sun comes through the windows. Instead, the wind batters against the house, and lightning streaks the early morning sky. The earthy smell of rain fills the house and mixes with the scent of animals.

The boy completes his chores and then he goes to the roof to wait.

He hears the cars arrive and peeps over the tiles to watch them park along the country street. The police are first, then the animal rescuers, and other normally dressed people with red number plates.

These are the ones he fears the most – the social workers.

There are six cars in total and a van. The people in them slowly make their way out and prepare themselves for invasion. They come in all different shades of uniforms, but he knows they have the same thoughts.

He stays on the roof and prays that Ted will stay quiet. The rain comes down hard now, and he worries about sliding off. The knock at the front door is louder than before.

He hears the same voice from yesterday. "Victoria Police. Open up!"

He doesn't respond, but he feels his animal heart beating hard in his chest. He hears the window being opened and then the footsteps inside the house. They move towards the front door.

"Time to move!" Ted screeches.

"Not yet."

The rain is coming down so hard now that it practically blinds him, but he waits until he hears everyone moving inside before he makes his descent.

He slides down the drain and lands deftly on his feet. He creeps around to the back first and lets the dogs in. Then he goes to the side windows, all winched open, and starts to pull the strings he put there the night before. These open all the doors in the house, and some are attached to buckets and pans – the loud crash wakes and rouses all the animals. The animals respond and start to move from their rooms. The cries and screeches start, human and animal alike. Then the boy makes his way to the front door. He opens it and takes in the scene inside.

He sees all the animals running free about the house. There is a kaleido-scope of coloured birds, their feathers fly around the room. The dogs run wild among the feathers, barking and yapping at the invaders.

But everyone seems to pause at his entry, the boy of feathers, drenched wet – a scrawny kid with a cockatoo on his shoulder. A boom of thunder sounds, followed by a flash of lightning behind him, as he stands at the door with his hands on his hips, taking in the scene inside. Everything goes quiet for a moment.

"Jesus Christ," one of the police officers mutters.

The boy howls like a wolf, and everything turns to chaos. Possums fly from the roof. Their branches are strewn about everywhere. The deep bark of the dogs and yaps from the little ones drown out most of the noise. Birds and feathers flap in every room. Ted makes his appearance from the boy's shoulder and shouts louder than the rest, "Time to go. Time to go. Time to go!"

It seems, for a while, that they might win.

But then the humans take over.

More doors fly open, and animals stream out. The makeshift blinds fall to the ground, and the light from outside comes through the windows to expose the deep decay of the house. Even the boy sees it clearer now, next to the cleanliness of the people inside.

Then the people trap the animals, and cages come out. The male police officer grabs the boy's ankle as he tries to escape with the animals. He misses, though, and the boy kicks back with a hiss and catches him in the jaw. The policeman stumbles backwards but soon moves forward to grab him again. This time, he makes contact and grips firmly onto the boy's ankle. The boy pulls away as hard as he can, and even Ted comes to his aid, screeching and flapping – but it is of no use.

The boy's eyes roam wild, taking in everything. He keeps trying to pull away, reaching for the window. If he can just make it to the trees, he will be okay. He can pull himself up on the bark, and things will be fine.

But the police officer is stronger than the boy. And he wins. The boy doesn't give up. He screeches like a bird and wiggles, flapping his arms. Then one of the animal rescuers speaks to him. She is short with blonde hair and reminds him of one of the Pomeranians. He hears one of the other workers call her Kate.

"It's time to stop, mate."

He bares his teeth at her and barks like a dog. She rears back but pushes on.

"I know you're afraid, but what are you fighting for?"

This makes him stop for a moment.

"Is it for them? Are you trying to save them?"

He nods slowly.

"If that's what you're trying to do, you need to look at them. Really look. Do you think they'll survive here like this?"

"I can't leave them."

For a moment, she seems shocked to hear him speak but nods her understanding.

"Just look at them though. I know you love them, and you've done a great job looking after them. But you can't do it by yourself anymore. We want to help."

The boy's chest moves up and down at a rapid pace, and he takes in all the animals, looking with fresh eyes. He sees the ribs on the dogs, the missing feathers on the birds – the diseases on their skin. Things he hadn't noticed. Not really.

He hangs his head and concedes the loss. He whistles low to the dogs, and they all come to attention and then sit at his feet. He uses his hands to hush the birds and calms them down. The humans watch on in amazement.

The boy walks outside into the sunshine. The storm has now passed. He can't bear to see the animals trapped. A social worker asks if he would like to pack some things, and he replies simply, "I have nothing." The female rescuer tries to put Ted in a cage, and the boy looks away, the pain too much. Then he hears the cage drop and feels the claws on his shoulder.

The female rescuer approaches. She looks at him with pity and tries to grab Ted, who snaps his strong beak at her.

"I think he is your protector."

The boy smiles. "He is."

"Maybe you have something to take with you after all." She smiles in return, and he understands.

The animals are all soon packed up, and the boy wearily climbs into a car belonging to one of the social workers. He watches the house of feathers grow smaller behind him – the home that is no more.

TOP TEN

STEVE EVANS

CRAIGBURN FARM, SA, AUSTRALIA

Steve Evans writes fiction, poetry and non-fiction. He has written or edited twenty-one books (nine of poetry), including Easy Money and Other Stories, *and the poetry collections* Unearthly Pleasures *and* Animal Instincts. *He has won and been shortlisted for various Australian and international prizes and was previously Head of English at Flinders University where he ran the Creative Writing Program.*

STORM

The house is a shattering of wind
and fleeing birds,
its windows shaking in their frames
played like drums in hail-shot rain
as if on the brink of collapse.

How fragile we are in here,
all night paper-thin and fearful,
startled by thundered light
that fractures our brief bravado at a whim
with camera flashes of stunned faces.

A calm will come, we know,
but there are hours to go,
and we could drown in these rooms,
insignificant as the electric air.

TOP TEN

GAYLE BEVERIDGE
BASS COAST, VIC, AUSTRALIA

Gayle Beveridge is an Aussie living on Victoria's beautiful Bass Coast. She is passionate about writing fiction, sunsets, chocolate, birdwatching and photography. Gayle's stories have been widely published, and some of these are in anthologies such as Award Winning Australian Writing, Mosaic, The Umbrella's Shade *and* Vegemite Whiskers.

THE LIGHTNING TRAVELLER

"Hey. Watch yourself."

Damien, startled by the odour of street grime and bad breath, was only vaguely aware someone had spoken to him. He'd been travelling again. That's what he liked to call it, travelling; his body just hanging about while his mind was off on some distant adventure.

"You alright, mate?"

He felt something on his arm and looked to it; a hand, all skinned knuckles and black-rimmed fingernails. It was large and knobbly, and Damien remembered his dad's hands, grown fat from a lifetime of swinging a hammer. This wasn't Dad though.

"Let go of me," he squeaked. He pulled away, nudging an older man beside him, and got a shove and a thump in the back for his troubles.

The hand steadied him. "You alright, mate? You've been stepping about all over; invading other people's space. Folks are trying to settle for the evening."

"Sorry." He looked up. The man was heavy, as wide as an ogre, with long tangled hair and a wild, wild beard. Damien saw a bird nesting in that beard, with wings the colours of a rainbow and golden all-seeing eyes, tugging and twining the hairy tendrils. There was something magic about that bird. If he could just touch it, run a finger along a feather, he knew, he just knew, he too would be able to fly. He reached for it, but his hand fell short, pushed back by powers unknown.

"I'm Rob. You got a name?" The ogre, having taken Damien's hand in his, waited. Not everybody on the street had a name. Some were running even from themselves.

Damien had a recollection of a beautiful bird, but looking about, saw none. He wondered why the stranger was holding his hand.

"Who are you?" he said.

"I'm Rob. What's your name?"

"Damien."

"Is this your first night out, then?" Ancient creases framed Rob's eyes, creases so old the dirt of the ages had settled in them.

Was this his first night out? Out where?

"I don't know," Damien said. But he knew he'd been travelling again. Best not to mention that; it unsettled people.

"C'mon." Rob pulled gently on Damien's hand. "The sandwich van will be down at the square in a couple of hours. If we get there early, we'll be at the front of the queue. I'll wager you could do with a feed."

As they walked, Damien noticed the cold tingle of drizzling rain on his skin. Tall buildings cast long, slender shadows. Night was not far away. They passed a department store, lines of windows, shiny products in flashy colours. Damien stopped where faceless mannequins with perfect bodies wore perfect dresses.

"Those dresses never fit that well," he said. "We pull them tight and pin them behind."

"You work there?" Rob asked.

"Used to," he replied, and relief settled on him. He was back. It always took a while to get properly back from the travelling.

"You got stuff somewhere?" Rob cast Damien a quizzical glance. "A sleeping bag, a coat maybe." The rain was heavier now. It carried a nip with it and spread it about in the air. Damien's T-shirt would offer little warmth.

"Stuff? No." Damien shook his head.

At the corner, they waited under a streetlight. Its yellow glow danced along Damien's arm and revealed faint brown markings, flowing from his shoulder like leafy tree branches. Rob nodded towards it.

"A bad tattoo you tried to get rid of?"

Damien smiled. People always thought it was a tattoo.

"I got hit by lightning, and it drew where it travelled. I guess it never wanted me to forget. There's a name for them, the scars, I mean, but I can't remember what it is."

"Christ, mate, you're lucky to be alive."

Was he lucky? Sometimes Damien wondered about that. The headlights of an oncoming car reflected on the wet road. So much light. Bright light. Coming closer. Getting brighter. Brighter than a thousand suns. Where had he heard that? A bomb! The flash of a nuclear bomb. Damien dropped to the ground and huddled behind a postbox, knees to his chest and arms wrapped around his head.

Somebody tugged on him.

"Get down," he screamed, but still they tugged. Too strong for him, they pulled him to his feet and shook him. He was a rag doll, his head lobbing this way and that. His thoughts tumbled and scattered, trying desperately to find the right place to settle.

"Damien," Rob called. "Damien. What the hell's wrong with you, mate? You on drugs or something?"

Drugs? Yes, he would need drugs for the radiation poisoning.

"Are you a doctor?" he asked, but as he said the words, somehow, they didn't sound right.

"What are you talking about? C'mon, mate, snap out of it."

"Mate," Damien repeated the word. This man must be a friend. The sun had dropped below the buildings, and dusk was drawing its blanket across the sleepy city. Where had the bright light gone? Damien was sure there had been bright light. Travelling. He had been travelling. He stood rigid, his eyes staring at nothing in particular. He was in that place where his thoughts were still trying to come home and sort themselves out.

Rob gave Damien's shoulder a couple of companionable thumps. "C'mon," he said. When he turned and walked, Damien followed. The kind master and the faithful puppy. As they went, a wall of grey cloud crept closer.

"How'd you come to be hit by lightning anyway?" Rob glanced at Damien, watchful now and wary of him. They walked a city block in silence. As they approached a crowd outside the theatre, the buzz and hum of conversation subsided. Folks in their finery recoiled, huddling with their companions, and they cleared a path for Rob and Damien so that they might not touch them.

Damien was properly back. "You ever play golf?"

Rob threw him a curious glance, and beneath tousled and greasy curls, the creases in his forehead scrunched.

"Golf? No, not my thing."

"Ginnie played," Damien said. "I was her caddy. I used to love those giant golf umbrellas. I wonder if they make them extra big so your clubs won't get wet. I had a black one with red writing. Ginnie loved colours though. She picked out a different one. It was orange and yellow and green. I didn't care much for it. Not a man's umbrella, you know."

"Right." Rob had slowed his pace.

"It had a wooden handle. That's what I was holding, but I was leaning that giant orange and yellow and green umbrella across my shoulder. The metal rod, well, that was pressing on my neck when the lightning came."

"Jesus, mate." Rob was shaking his head.

"Knocked me fair onto my knees," said Damien. "I don't remember much after that. Not until the hospital, at any rate. But what I do remember – and it's a crazy thing – you know how first you get the lightning and then the thunder? It wasn't like that. They both came at once." Damien rubbed his arm, running his hand back and forth along the tree-branch scar.

"Just a couple more blocks to the square," said Rob. "They'll give you a coffee with your sandwiches, and you can get some warmth into you."

"It's alright. I don't mind the cold so much." Damien rubbed his arm again. "It's the scar, it's tingling, like thousands of hot needle pricks. There's a storm coming."

Rob looked up, pushing sodden hair from his face. The moon had risen. It was a full moon, but it struggled to be seen, and was little more than a soft backlight to rolling clouds. "I reckon you're right," he said.

"I don't much like storms, Rob." Damien was in a forest. Tree branches whipped in a savage wind, and hailstones lashed at his flesh. The night was black as pitch, and unable to discern a way forward, he stumbled from tree to tree, scratching his arms and face against rough and ragged bark. Screams rose above the roar of thunder, animal screams, or perhaps his own. He called to the mountain wizard, and the wizard came. He took Damien by the hand and led him along a secret path.

When he was properly back, Damien was sitting with Rob on bluestone stairs in a sheltered doorway. This is my friend, he thought, and he sighed. There had been too much travelling today. It was the storm. Storms always derailed him. But today was different too. Here was his friend Rob, who had not gone away when the travelling started.

"Hey," he said.

"Hey," Rob replied. "What's going on with you, with this passing in and out of a daze? There something wrong with your head?"

"It was the lightning. It scrambled the circuits in my brain. Got them all mixed up and turned around. It's like my thoughts are always trying to put themselves right, and when they can't, they go searching, and they take me travelling with them."

"And this Ginnie, the golfer. What happened to her?"

"She tried, but it was too much for her. She said the Damien she knew died that day. She stuck around for a while. Duty more than love, I think. But

I couldn't work anymore. I lost my job, then the house."

"We've all got a story," said Rob. "The van's going to open soon. Let's get a sandwich and a drink."

They were sipping their coffees, making them last, when the lightning flashed. It forked above the buildings. Once. Twice. Three times. Damien knew the enemy was near, but still it had caught him off-guard. He saw the flash of artillery fire before he heard its roar. Would the guns never stop? He threw himself into the trenches, with his hands over his ears pressing tighter and tighter, but they were no barrier to the sound. How much more could he endure? Yet, in this darkest of times, he felt a presence in the trenches. He forced himself to look. A man, heavyset and as wide as an ogre, with long, tangled hair and a wild, wild beard. In Damien's mind, a few thoughts, just a few, put themselves right.

"This is my friend Rob," he told himself, and in the damp and muddy dirt of the trench, with the lice and the rats and the rot, came an inkling that this might not be real.

TOP TEN

JENNIFER HARRISON
WINDSOR, VIC, AUSTRALIA

Jennifer Harrison has published eight poetry collections. Her ninth collection, Sideshow History, *is forthcoming in 2023 from Black Pepper, Melbourne. She received the 2012 Christopher Brennan Award for sustained achievement in Australian poetry and is the current Chair of the World Psychiatric Association's Section for Art and Psychiatry.*

SHELTER

I put the key in the door
to unlock our dark peaceful home
and see terrible clouds in the wall
as if a barrier can no longer

block out the world –
I was surprised to need
a retreat or a cave against heaven
but then the clouds fell down the walls

subsiding in a puddle on the floor
as if there could no longer
be a boundary between inside
and outside

between botany and human –
from now on we gaze together
into habitat
disregarding the scientific rules

that have separated identity
from our names –
the idea of home an irretrievable privilege:
shell   web   den   nursing home

TOP TEN

PATRICIA FITZGERALD
QUEENSLAND, AUSTRALIA

Patricia's writing journey commenced some eight years ago at The Writer's Toy Box at U3A in Brisbane. During Covid, via Zoom, a small group of writers continued to explore different genres and encourage each other to traverse boundaries. Patricia writes to connect with her inner self and the planet surrounding her.

STORM IN A TEACUP

All around him, the storm raged. It was connected to his inner soul, his life force – who he was – and presented as an identity.

She had passed, screaming. Her essence sucked out of her as she birthed new life. Her eyes screamed with pain as she looked at Anna for the first and final time. Then with a whispered sigh, her soul was released.

THE CALL-UP

He felt he needed to go. He only had a small boat, but it could fit in two soldiers. Hopefully two lives could be saved.

He dragged the boat down the sharp-shelled beach, his boots leaving crunching footprints behind. The water was like ice milling around his legs as he thrust the boat forward and threw himself onto the seat.

His oilskin kept the worst of the rain away, though it was difficult to see past the penetrating mist.

Surrounding him was a flotilla of small craft. Neighbours and friends who had answered the call. There were no greetings or acknowledgement; everyone was focused on the distant shore and the men who waited.

The small sail held fast in the wind, and years of experience held the tiller at just the right angle to make as fast a trip as possible.

The beach approached, and he could see soldiers desperately crowding the waterway.

He headed towards two soldiers who were a little to the right. They clambered in, falling to the bottom of the boat, bloodied, soaked and exhausted.

THE RECLUSE

He was known in the neighbourhood as a recluse. Stories abounded that he had once been married, but many believed that was hearsay.

A couple of times a week, he ventured out in his old truck and headed off through the town to the wharf where his small boat was moored. When well away from land, he would take out his fishing tackle and the worms he had dug up that morning, and cast out his line.

Sometimes, he would just sit with the baitless hook in the water, his face raised upwards, and his fist punching a hole through God. These times, Gareth felt incredibly alone, and he would return to shore with an empty basket and an empty soul.

The only other time he left the house was on Christmas Day when he drove to the Catholic Church and parked in the gravel laneway.

He always sat on the back pew, right on the aisle. If anyone else was sitting there, they edged themselves away to a respectable distance. The children would send inquisitive yet uneasy glances in his direction, and the mums and dads would shoosh them and guide them back to the ministrations of the priest.

After the service, Gareth would extend his hand to Father Rudd and, without any further acknowledgement, walk back down the laneway and return home.

WALLS BEGIN TO CRUMBLE

The Christmas following Dunkirk, Gareth's routine altered slightly.

He moved towards the front of the church and sat next to a family with four children. They glanced up at him with surprise, though the wife managed a tight half-smile.

Afterwards, he wandered to the corner of the church where the Nativity Scene lay. He stood for an exceptionally long time, looking at the baby in the crib. Eventually, a few silent tears trickled down his cheek, and he turned away.

Father Rudd was waiting for him in the doorway as he entered the sunlight. He grasped Gareth's hand and invited him for a cup of tea with the congregation. Gareth, once again, graciously declined. As he turned to leave, he found his way blocked by Mary, Lisbet's best friend, her face cracking a wide smile.

"Hello, Mary."

Mary beamed. "It's so lovely to see you, Gareth. Are you coming to the hall for morning tea?"

"I have other plans," he spluttered as he edged away.

The smile faded on Mary's face, and something in her eyes moved him.

He had never stopped to think how Lisbet's death may have affected anyone else. He had been selfishly wrapped up in his own loss and self-pity.

Mary's pain was obviously as raw as his own. With an uncharacteristic smile he said, "My plans can wait half an hour. Let's have a cuppa."

They wandered into the hall together. Gareth kept his head down, trying to avert making eye-contact. Mary chatted on, but he only heard her in a haze. The walls were closing in on him, and after a quick cuppa and a slice of fruit cake, he took his leave.

THE STORM

The following Sunday, he headed out to sea in his small boat. A storm had been predicted, but he didn't care. As the waves gradually increased, he expertly flew over the peaks and slipped through the furrows.

The waves crashed down onto him, and he abandoned himself to the elements, tears of ice forming on his skin.

The relentless wind caught the sail and ripped it apart. The mast was in danger of snapping.

He thought about his beautiful Lisbet and his long-lost child. Lisbet would have gently chided him over his self-imposed isolation. She was someone who had loved life. She would have expected him to move on.

With an extreme effort, Gareth took back control of the crippled boat. The sea resisted, fighting back and throwing everything at him. Waves crashed around, and the boat was tossed like a cork. Slowly, he fought back to shore and into the safety of the harbour, where he securely tethered the small sailboat.

Wet, bedraggled and half-drowned, he dragged himself over to his truck. As if in a dream, he found himself outside Mary's cottage. He walked up the pathway and, after a moment's hesitation, gave a couple of firm knocks on the door. As the door opened, he smiled.

"Is there a spare cup of tea in the pot?"

TOP TEN

RIYA PATEL

NEW JERSEY, UNITED STATES

Riya Patel is a seventeen-year-old fiction writer who has written fantasy short stories and speculative flash fiction. Currently, she is exploring screenwriting and working on a few short scripts.

A BREEZE THAT BROUGHT IN A TAXI CAB

In a New York City apartment, an infant cries in his crib. His mother, in the kitchen, struggles to wash the mountain of dishes piled in the sink while balancing a phone between her ear and shoulder. A plate slips from her hands, falling back into the soapy water. A small backsplash bounces up, sprinkling the mother's face.

"I'm gonna have to call you back, Marge."

She tosses the sponge on the counter, then wipes her hands with the towel hanging from the oven handle. She glances over her shoulder to check the time flashing blue on the microwave – 10:47 pm. With a sigh, she begins down the hallway towards the wailing infant.

A flick of the switch illuminates the room, a room vibrant with toys sprawled on the crayon-stained carpet, mellowed by the pastel blue walls and shelves of stuffed animals. Upon hearing footsteps, the infant reaches up with his fat fingers and lets out another squeal, waiting for his mother's arms to scoop him up, and the mother does just that. She holds the baby tight against her chest, gently bobbing her arms until the cries subside.

As she waits, a breeze slips in from the open window, drying out the mother's already tired eyes. Raindrops patter against the windowsill, seeping into the apartment. The mother waits for her son to fall asleep to the gentle rhythm of the drizzle outside. Then, with gentle hands, she lays him back in his crib, where his eyes flutter under his lids, active and dreaming, his chest continuing to rise and fall as it rains outside.

Slowly, the mother pushes the window closed, careful to avoid any harsh squeaking that would wake the infant. Outside, a rapid movement catches her eye. A young woman flails her hand towards the street. The headlights of a bright yellow taxi flash, illuminating her body for a moment, then rush past her, splashing her from the puddles formed from the falling rain. The mother smiles – not at the woman's misfortune, but at the memory of her own youth. A youth that ended abruptly just thirteen months ago.

Suddenly, the rain outside turns into a downpour, soaking the sidewalk cement a shade darker and the woman's clothes a layer sheerer. The mother debates opening the window back up and calling out to the woman, but what would she say? If she were better, maybe she would offer the woman shelter in the apartment, but she couldn't risk waking her son. So instead, the mother watches as the woman huddles within her bomber jacket under a dim lamppost.

Water drips from the sill into a small puddle on the hardwood floor. The problem, the mother decides, is for tomorrow, and she switches the lights off and leaves for her own bed. She falls stomach-first onto the soft comforter, not bothering to change out of her jeans, barely unclipping the clasps of her bra. She inhales the faint smell of laundry detergent from the scarcely used sheets and pulls several layers of blankets over her body.

Outside, a bolt of lightning flashes, a low rumble of thunder following milliseconds after. From one room over, the infant cries from his crib.

TOP TEN

JACQUELINE WINN

POSSUM BRUSH, NSW, AUSTRALIA

Jacqueline Winn lives on a farm at Possum Brush on the east coast of Australia. Her short stories have been awarded and published in Australia, New Zealand and UK. Ginninderra Press has published two collections of her stories, Once More with Feeling *and* Salt & Pepper. *For more information, visit www.jacquelinewinn.com*

WHEN GOD GOES MAD

Tania tells me she's God. Big G or little g, I'm not really sure. She drops it into the conversation, amongst her rambling burble of thoughts, half-started, never finished. She's in the throes of one of those whirling tempests that hold her mind hostage every couple of months or so. Though, in recent times, the periods of calm seem to be getting shorter, the storms more frequent.

Declaring she's God is not a new thing for Tania, so the whole time she's babbling, I'm waiting for her to say it. Even then, the assertion never fails to surprise. God, eh? Those are the words inside my head, but I don't say it aloud in case it comes across as impolite, uncaring even. Being God is an awfully big idea, but she never offers any reasoning, no elaboration or anecdotal evidence. She just puts it out there. With her face too close to mine, she fixes her raw unblinking eyes on me, making sure I get it. Except I don't.

She's drunk. Smells like she hasn't showered in days, and her teeth are so furred I'm wondering if I shouldn't offer her the use of a toothbrush. None of this is unusual. For years, she's been arriving at my back door, giggling, unsteady, except for the hand holding an overfull glass of red. How she ever manages to squeeze through the gap in the fence without spilling any is a miracle in itself. Perhaps she really is God. No, that's an unkind thought, flippant. She doesn't deserve that.

Mostly, her visits are late afternoon, just before the kids come home from school. For Tania, it's that moment when the day behind her becomes overwhelming and the arrival of two noisy teenagers threatens to tip it right over the edge.

Recently, though, she's been making the whole thing easier on herself, arriving at my door early, bringing the wine cask along with her glass. She has no intention of sharing. I can't imagine what she'd say if I took out a glass and held it out for her to fill. She might give me a sip or two, but I suspect she'd make some excuse to fob me off.

"You're my best neighbour," she tells me.

Truth is, I'm her only neighbour. Well, the only one who hasn't quit the field, the only one who hasn't told her to sober up, get some counselling, before shutting the door in her face. I might be the last one standing, but being Tania's best neighbour is not a matter of kindness on my part, necessarily. I'm just a bit gutless when it comes to saying what needs to be said, and on top of that, a tiny bit worried. If she can't come here, where can she go? I'm not much of a backstop, but at least I might be able to stop the slide just a little.

"You're my friend," she goes on. "That's why I can tell you I'm God. I know you'll understand."

Wrong again. I have no idea what she means by that. Any friendship I've offered in the past certainly hasn't helped so far. I'm way out of my depth, and every time she turns up, I'm just gritting my teeth, trying to figure out a way to dodge around all her weird ideas and see if I can't convince her to go home and sleep it off.

She's just finished another of her God moments when she asks me the time. I check my watch and tell her it's a little after two.

"Shit!" she says. "I've got an appointment."

Fantastic, I'm thinking. She's only been here half an hour – must be my lucky day.

But she pulls me up with, "Can you drive me? Dunno where my keys are. Haven't seen 'em for days."

I'm nodding my head, smiling at her and giving the impression I'm happy to help out. Stupid, but I just can't say no. In fact, I know where her keys are, and so does she. Her husband takes them to work every day to make sure she doesn't drive while drunk. And he's been doing it a lot longer than a few days. He's told her to take the bus if she needs to go anywhere, but the local bus drivers know her and won't pick her up in case she throws up on the bus again. If I don't give her a lift, she's stuck.

"What sort of appointment?" I ask while tying up my runners. Hopefully, a doctor's appointment. That would be really handy right now. I wouldn't mind the chance to get her to a doctor, especially while she's at her worst. A doctor would know how to deal with all this crazy stuff, for sure.

"Hairdresser," she says.

Disappointed doesn't tell the half of it. But I swallow it down, grab my bag, herd her out through the front door. I'm barely in the driver's seat when I notice she's toting the wine cask. She's put the glass down somewhere, but she's not leaving that cask behind. I could tell her she can't take it in the car, but I'm not sure she'll take kindly to me coming between her and a drink. She who runs away lives to fight another day, that's my motto, so I ignore her. As I'm pulling out of the driveway, she's jiggling the cask around on her lap and fiddling with the tap. I reckon it'll be only minutes before she's sneaking it up to her lips.

Wrong about the minutes. Only seconds later, I'm mustering my nicest sidelong glare as she lifts the cask and gives the tap a quick suck. The glare is lost on her, and I chastise myself for allowing nice to get in the way of necessity again.

Of course, when we get to the hairdressers, the wine cask comes in with us, clutched under her arm like a handbag. She announces her arrival by dumping it with a loud smack on the reception desk. When she announces she has a booking, the young apprentice tells her, "I'm sorry, Mrs Copeman, we don't seem to have an appointment for you."

Tania laughs – shrieks, to be more accurate. "You can fit me in." Then she calls out to the senior hairdresser, who is drying the hair of a client at the back of the salon. "Hey, Susie! Just a quick cut."

The poor flustered apprentice looks over her shoulder at three women sitting in the waiting area, before trying again. "Um, we're a bit booked out. I'll just ask Sue if—"

But Tania's not waiting for permission. She's already swung her cask off the reception desk, toddled over to one of the vacant cutting chairs and claimed a spot. She slips in another swig before placing the cask on the shelf in front of her. Not too far from reach.

"I'm sorry," I mutter to the young girl.

In seconds, Tania starts yelling, "Right, Susie, I want it cut really short. My husband likes it long, so cut it as short as you can go. That'll fix him."

"I'm so sorry," I repeat a little louder.

From the back of the salon, Sue cuts me off with an understanding nod and beckons the apprentice to come over. She gives the girl a couple of quick instructions on finishing her client's blow-dry, then goes to stand behind Tania's chair.

"How are you, Tania?" Sue's pleasant tone is impressive as she swirls the black cape around Tania and secures it at the back of her neck.

I can't imagine how irritating this must be. Though, maybe it's not the first time Sue has seen Tania in one of these maelstrom moments. Maybe she knows to tackle it head on, get the job done as fast as possible and see her out the door before too many waiting clients desert their seats.

"How am I?" Tania's voice is so loud a couple of the waiting women wince at the onslaught. "Shit, if you must know. Absolute shit."

"Right, so you'd like me to cut it short?" Sue presses on regardless, and as she picks up the scissors and comb, she passes me a little wave of her hand, as if to say it's okay, we'll deal with it.

I don't know if Tania spotted the gesture, but she throws her head in my direction, yelling, "That's my friend Julie, my best neighbour. She believes in me. She believes I'm God."

It's one of those please-let-the-earth-swallow-me-up moments. Every head in the salon turns towards me, as if I'm the one responsible for bringing the mad woman here, the one who's standing around doing nothing to stop the whole wrecking ball crashing into the unsuspecting crowd.

Tania shrieks again, pulling every eye back in her direction. "And you believe in me as well, don't you, Susie? You believe I'm God."

The hairdresser is too slow to answer, and Tania pounces on it. Her voice pushes up another thunderous notch. "Yeah, I get it. You don't believe me, do you? None of you fuckers believe me."

She pulls her head away from the snipping scissors, knocking the comb to the floor. As Sue ducks to retrieve it, Tania leaps out of the chair. She frantically flaps the black cape aside, making a grab for a jar of scissors on the shelf. They clatter to the floor, and she scrabbles around until she's got a grip on one pair. Then she presses herself under the shelf, back against the wall, legs drawn up, one hand held high, pointing the scissors at all comers.

"Dare me!" she screams. "Come close, go on. Dare me!"

My feet are moving well before I can even think, and I find myself standing in front of Sue, my arms spread wide as if to protect her. Good grief, what on earth am I doing? There's a pair of sharp scissors pointing straight at me, and I suddenly realise I must be as crazy as Tania to imagine best neighbour or best friend counts for anything right now.

"Tania," I say as softly as I can. "It's okay."

Geez, what am I saying? It's far from okay, and I'm desperately hoping that little beeping sound I can hear from somewhere behind me is someone phoning for the police, an ambulance, whoever it is you need to call in this kind of situation. But I can't afford to look around, can't afford to check. I need to hold Tania's wild eyes, scary as that is. I can hear the front door faintly squeaking back and forth. Everyone is getting out while they can, and the scurry of feet behind me says the apprentice and the other clients have made their own getaway as well.

Sue is still there right behind me, thank goodness. I can hear her breathing steadily, and when she takes a small step back, I follow suit. She's thinking a lot straighter than I am. Putting some distance between the scissors and us is a sensible move.

Tania is sobbing now, shaking with the grief of it all, but her hand is still outstretched, her knuckles white with their grip on the scissors.

"Can you give me the scissors, Tania?" I ask in a tiny voice. I'm not sure how this will help, seeing as there are a half-dozen pairs scattered around her on the floor. Retrieve one, and she can easily pick up another.

Sue chips in over my shoulder, "Would you like a cup of tea, Tania? Might make you feel better."

My first thought is no, please don't leave me alone with her. Don't go off and make a cup of tea and leave me guessing what to do next. But Tania stops crying for a moment, then nods and starts to lower her hand. It's almost as if she's forgotten we're the enemy, as if the cup of tea idea has started to move things back to something closer to calm.

Sue starts to step away towards the tearoom, tiptoeing as if any careless movement might topple the situation back the other way.

I'm breathing a little easier now, convinced Tania is about to let the scissors drop to the floor. But then, without so much as a shred of warning, her fingers twist around, and she sweeps her hand up to her neck, pressing the awful point against the soft skin just beneath her ear.

"Shh!" I hush urgently. "Shh, come on, Tania, you need to put the scissors down."

She's quaking with sobs again, rocking back and forth, and there's a real danger she'll stab herself whether she wants to or not.

"Shh!" I hush again, dropping to a crouch, shuffling towards her as gently as I can. "Shh!" I keep repeating it, not because I think it might help, but because I have no idea what I'm supposed to say.

She stops rocking for a moment, turns a face of complete misery on me and wails, "You believe me, don't you, Julie?"

"Yes, Tania." I'm happy to lie as much as she needs. "Of course, I do. I believe you."

"I'm God," she says. "Aren't I?"

"Yes, you are. You're just having a bad day, that's all."

Goodness knows where that last bit came from, but the instant she hears it, the scissors tumble out of her hand and clatter onto the floor. I grab them, along with every other damn sharp implement lying anywhere within her reach, and toss them all across the room as far as I can. Then I squeeze under the shelf beside her, wriggle an arm around her shoulders and just hold her.

Sue comes back with a cup of tea, puts it in Tania's trembling hands, then goes to wait near the door. There's a siren in the distance, and a small crowd has gathered around the salon clients outside. No doubt, they're asking all those none-of-their-business questions, passing on a wealth of ill-informed opinions.

We stay sitting under the shelf while Tania sips the tea, her sobs calming little by little, as if the storm is heading out to sea at last. With my arm still around her shoulder, I don't say anything. I've never been much good at finding the right words when they're needed.

When the ambulance paramedics walk in, I breathe a huge sigh of relief. It's over, and hopefully, it's the start of getting some help for Tania at last. Though I have to confess to feeling awful for not doing something long before it came to this.

Just before they help her into the ambulance, Tania gives me a hug, squeezes me half to death. I'd like to think I'm a good friend, a good neighbour. It's just that I'm a bit clueless, a bit hopeless at dealing with things like this. After all, it's a slippery business when God goes mad.

2

STORMY PLACES

KETCHUM BAY

BEVERLEY LELLO

This small bay was possessed, seething and
churning until the storm passed, smudging
a giant thumbprint of bruised grey on the horizon.
In its wake, the waters toss and spike,

curled lips of froth plunging shoreward. Thick,
gritty sea foam is piled high, slapped on the cold,
wet sand and left stranded as the water sucks in
its breath and retreats to harvest more.

Our footprints mark this shore, kick at the foam.
The wind lifts it, and we watch it scud and eddy,
disperse, dissolve, dematerialise. Dishevelled clumps
of brown, slippery-as-eels seaweed, like the tangled hair

of Medusa, strangle our boots as we scramble
across the rocks, crab-like clinging, climbing down
onto another bay clogged with the same brown scunge
and restless, wrathful waves.

Four days pass. We return. The sea is serene,
the beach scoured clean. Gentle waves lap the shore.
The white foam bubbles and sinks into the sand
and pocks the place that drew it in. Our footsteps

are swallowed as we leave the beach and climb
onto the ridge above. When we look back,
the sky is blue, the sand a pale gold and the water
mute, a sliver of mirror framed by trees.

STORM OVER PRIMROSE PARK

SHALE PRESTON

I pull into the parking spot
where I used to take my mother
to look at the water and eat takeaway
we never got out of the car
just wound the windows down
breathed in the hot air and looked across
at the overturned row boats on the shoreline
beneath the tri-level houses with "commanding" views

it has just started to rain and the cricket players
are deserting the pitch
ripping off their pads and running for cover
as gunmetal clouds race across the sky
cockatoos dive for branches then hang from them
like extra-large Christmas tree baubles
raindrops hit the windscreen heavily
threatening to become something more
I debate driving off but the thunder is insistent
the lightning imperious

if my mother were with me
I'd tell her that
it's best to stay put until it's over
but her name's on a bronze memorial plaque
with a rose bud border
so I cover the windscreen with a foldable reflective visor
then put my chair back and close my eyes
as water drips down
from the duct-tape-sealed sunroof

ON NEWTOWN BRIDGE

COLLEEN Z BURKE

Yesterday
flimsy clouds
barely dimmed
the intensity
of blue soaring
overhead

But today
storms ravage
wintry skies
as clouds
blistered with
light slip over
the edge

STORM OVER LAKE ALEXANDRINA

JUDE AQUILINA

Milang, South Australia

All afternoon
a howling south-easterly
pipes whitecaps
of icing over the lake.
Jetty-bound seagulls
plant feet like tiny tree roots
clawing into wet wood.

Town windows and doors
are bolted shut, awnings torn,
washing lines stripped,
as rattled locals listen inside.

Streetlight eyes open early
trying to brighten the murky day
but rain weakens
their myopic stares.

A dirty snowbank of papers
and plastic bags
rises against a mesh fence.
Louvres sing their old song.
Sailors say thank you prayers.

Restless, boofy gusts
puff their bravado
on this edgy evening.
Narrung's thugs
have blown in
from across the lake
to rule the streets
of Milang.

3

PEOPLE & STORMS

WESTERLIES

PETER FRANKIS

This story was written on unceded Wodi Wodi land

Wednesday was brisk, and by evening, it had started to howl. Everything clanked and squealed and slammed and banged and eased and banged again. Come daylight, it was a full-faced gale. Clouds raced across the sky, and the sea was silver, water going straight up into the air.

Then about four in the afternoon, the wind fell into a hole, and suddenly, it had become just an ordinary winter's afternoon. Ordinary, except everything was clean. All our rubbish, the stuff of our lives, the households on the side of the road – busted highchairs, vinyl lounges, carpet rolls – gone, simply blown away.

Aside from a row of downed pines and a house with a peeled-back roof (the guy gives me a wave from between the rafters), it was a postcard. I walked down to the sea and watched as it nudged the polished sand, gulls preening and bickering. It was as if nothing had happened.

But there were odd things: arrowed into a fence was an envelope with a strange address, an interstate postcode; a kid's book splayed on the grass, big colourful drawings, a furious tiger rounding a palm tree, but the words were nonsense, written in some foreign language; a handbag jagged in a tree; a pair of high heels; and a silver wig spilling out like the pelt of some frosted marsupial.

The gale must've snatched this stuff right out of their hands.

I was saying this at dinner, "Who are these people?"

"It's like Pompeii," she replied.

"All those stones," she mused. "Remember? And that train."

The Circumvesuviana back to Naples – tourists, students, housewives, teachers, everyone pressed in close, the heat, their breath, sweat, groceries. The lovers in the back, kissing. The girl arched her back. He said how bad he wanted her. The sway of the train, the beat of their hips, and all of us vanished, along with the paddocks and vineyards out the window. Just the two of them.

"Remember back when we couldn't keep our hands off each other?" She laughed. "There was nothing outside our bedroom."

She puts her wine down and gives me one of her looks.

"That was years ago," I said. "And I'm too old." Truth was, I couldn't recall any of that.

Later, I'm dreaming. There's a weight pressing me down, gentle at first but definite, then inexorable, fixing me here forever. My hands push at the sheets, and I wake up gasping, convinced the house, the hall, is filled with sand. But there's only our bedroom, the sound of her sleeping and the wind picking up again.

COCKROACH, HONEY

STEVE EVANS

They play country classics on this station,
she says, slowly scratching her damp neck
as I count moths on the screen.

She smells of the bitter stuff
we smear on our wrists to ward off the
biting insects at dusk.

Doesn't nobody ever want to
just roll in that stink of themselves and each
other like melted butter, she laughs.

I don't know how long we kept it going, but
I finally say, you better put on your clothes,
and I pick up my keys.

Do I really have to?
There's a storm coming, she says,
and I get so sticky in this heat.

Let's stay a while, and you tell me about
how I make your skin just sing, but first,
won't you kill that cockroach, honey?

IN THE HARSH OF WINTER

SUZI MEZEI

Under ruptured sky   the car rides
    a grey slick of freeway,
the final stretch of open   space
before ice storms churn half-formed streets
        to mires,
and the smallness of your house
    crowds in on us.
An electric crack begins at the top
of your world, tumbles through clouds and lands
at the place where   *he*   taught you to follow;
    never to lead.
I stand beneath a naked bulb wired loose
    to the eaves, its glow fragile,   trapped
at concrete angles. You tether dogs
and children, open the door in yesterday's clothes,
the print of his thumbs still etched on the soft
    of your neck. You invite me inside a squall
of his making, lives strewn like crumpled papers,
sapling sons   warped from the asymmetry he taught;
watchful, well-versed in the art of anger, quick learners.

Your broken rabble, hollow   howling
loud as a gale, your voice gusted in and   out
of sparse rooms, thin as tumbleweed, an echo
picked up and dropped hard as you fling a few things
in plastic bags   *He's gone*   you say.
            For now, for now the thunder retorts,
the thump of it heavy as rhythmic fists
on the drowned roof. You collect your cigarettes,
some toys, herd those you love,   cut ties
with all that's   left behind,
            you   stare   the tempest   in its dark eye,
let hail pile like frigid pearls   in your wake
on the ragged trek   to freedom.

THE VISIT

LEONE GABRIELLE

A wet knock in a rainstorm. It's tattooed Chaos in baggy chic. Hardened, lean, saturated. Teeth removed. Eyes in pirate sockets. Chaos is an ex-neighbour from my thorny street.

"You!" I say.

He smiles. "Just got out."

We watch each other, me on the green couch, him under the cold light of the south window.

"I'm house bitching, at my oldest, no appreciation," he says.

I do not offer a cup of tea. He does not stop for breath. I nod politely at his business ventures. Sheets of sliding water on the window obscure a bird who sits pelted. Rain dents, then falls off soft, dark feathers. The old fodder tree, a thousand arms raging in an electric frenzy.

Chaos gets up, sits down, gets up, inspects every room of my leaking house, all the while lecturing on Victorian prisons, stabbings, resurrected parents. His real interest, we both know, some cash – a ten.

Windy waters colonise the garden. Perched on a pitchfork's welded handle, this bird pivots its head. The rain hardens, and yellow-ringed eyes stare straight into mine.

"I heard Matty moved to Melbourne," I say, leading Chaos towards the front door and sliding him a note.

"Na!" he says. "He's in witness protection. I cut his finger off. He's in Shep."

I closed the door. I hadn't asked which …

In my dark room, I watch nature's colours slide. Fat raindrops hit the pied currawong; its beak oscillates, left, right, tapping the air. The wind is up. The carport's truss ignored. I swallow. White rain hacks into the yard's towering eucalyptus. In swirling branches, cockies, crows and magpies fluster, then become obscure.

My nose is pressed to the cold. I'm fogging up the window, wish-whispering to myself. The bird springs up, collects a piece of kitchen scrap, hops onto an apple branch, looks around and ascends into the tempest.

THE CLOUDS ABOVE US

PERRY NARBOROUGH

The clouds were boiling above as the son stumbled over the last few metres of the track. He emerged from the bush, surrounded by the grassy plains of the camp site. It was dark at the bottom of the valley, and the few boulders that lay strewn across the site were covered in moss. He unclipped his chest straps and looked around. The late afternoon sun was fading, but he could make out his mother and father in the distance, sitting on camp chairs under a tarp next to the tent. It seemed they were the only ones here.

His father spotted him and waved. "Looks like it's gonna be pissing down soon!" he called out and walked over, holding out a packet of chips. "You two are gonna have fun setting up your tent." His words echoed in the quiet camp site. "Where's James?"

The son took off his hat.

"He's behind, but he's coming."

The father swatted away a mosquito flying near his neck.

"What do you mean?"

The son took off his pack and placed it by his feet. He looked around the clearing as he spoke.

"I went off ahead. But he knows where he's going – we both had a map." Thunder rolled in from the distance. The boy looked around again. "He had blisters, and we just thought I could go on ahead . . . y'know, to help set up the tent." He looked up at the swirling clouds outlined in the deep green of a summer storm.

"What?"

"Well . . . I . . . we just thought since you two went ahead, I could come and help too."

"Your mum and I left together. We left you and James together."

"It's only since lunchtime, so he can't be that—"

"Lunch?" The father turned around and started walking back to the tent. The son picked up his pack and jogged to catch up to him. The sun was setting fast now, the shadows in the valley slowly fading into the obscurity of twilight. Thunder rumbled across the skyline once more, louder this time.

"Christ."

"Dad, he can't be that far—"

The father stopped and turned to him. "Do you know how hard it is to find someone in the dark?" The hint of panic put an edge to his father's words.

The father turned back and continued to the tent. The son stood in the middle of the grassy expanse. He saw his mother stand up and talk to his dad. He dropped his pack down once more. The summer air was rich and heavy, carrying with it the scent of rain.

The son shook his head, convincing himself of something. Thunder in the distance echoed throughout the valley.

*   *   *   *   *

The rising sun set the clouds on the horizon in a deep orange. It reflected off the ocean, glimmering in the surf.

"Might rain later."

"What?"

James had his arms crossed and shoulders hunched against the fresh morning air. He stared into the distance as the older brother was trying to stuff his sleeping bag into his pack.

"I'm beginning to think Mum and Dad just left early to avoid helping us pack up."

James kept staring over to the clouds in the distance.

The older brother finally closed his pack. It bulged in places it seemed it shouldn't. He picked up the towels lying next to it and slung one of them over his shoulder. He passed the other to James.

"You ready?" he asked.

They were alone as they wandered down to the beach – the other campers at the site had probably set off to avoid the worst of the sun. Yet the sand was cold as they waddled over the dunes, their thongs sinking into the sand as they went. James stopped as he stepped onto firm sand near the edge of the water.

"I don't know if I want to," he said.

"What? Why?"

"It's kinda cold."

The older brother squinted into the sunrise. "What do you mean? How often are you able to wake up by the ocean and go for a swim."

James nodded as he stared out to the surf, a fine ocean mist swirling around them like dust motes. The gentle crash of waves filled the silence.

"You definitely won't be able to do this in three months." The older brother paused and closed his mouth.

"Do you . . . know what you want to do yet?"

James kept staring.

"It's gotta be in by the end of the month, right?"

A wave went over their feet, the sand beneath them shifting.

"I might go back," said James. "It's kinda cold."

The older brother opened his mouth to say something, but James was already heading back.

He dropped his towel on the sand. The wind was picking up, and a sudden gust made him shiver. He looked at the figure in the distance walking back to the camp site. He turned back to the surf. The glow of sunrise was draining, leaving the clouds on the horizon a stale grey.

*　　*　　*　　*　　*

The son came over to where his mother was sitting, his father rifling through the tent behind her. The father emerged with a smaller knapsack and head torch.

"I'm going to head up the trail to see if he's close."

"What if he's not?" the mother asked.

The father fiddled with the straps on the head torch.

"I'll come too," said the son.

"No, you'll stay with your mother." The father tightened the torch onto his head and swung the pack over his shoulders.

"I've got a head torch too, I can—"

"Use your brain. We've already lost one – we don't need to lose another."

The father opened his map and consulted it. The mother held her gaze at the bush behind them.

"He's not lost. He's probably close," the son offered. "It's not like he hasn't hiked before."

The father turned to him, the shadows on his face accentuated by the clinical white light of the head torch.

"How would you know?"

The son said nothing.

"He doesn't have a phone; it's nearly pitch black, and a storm's heading in as we speak."

The son's cheeks felt hot even in the humid summer night air. He turned to his mother, but she held her gaze into the darkness.

The father left, heading across the grass towards the trail. His light bobbed as he walked, his figure nearly indiscernible in the late twilight. The son followed him.

Birds in distant treetops called out the threat of a storm.

*   *   *   *   *

The older brother felt his breathing pick up, and he concentrated on not slipping over on the dry dirt of the old fire trail. The ground was steeper now, and each step sent small rocks tumbling behind them.

"Can we stop for a sec?" James asked from behind.

"We're nearly there."

But by the time the older brother had turned around, James had already taken off his pack and was sitting in the dirt. The fire trail had led them out of the valley, and they had already climbed a fair distance in the half hour they had been walking. They were towering over the coast they had not so long ago set off from.

James shucked off his boots. "I think I got some blisters," he said, peeling off his socks.

The older brother looked over the valley. "Check out the view," he said, waving his drink bottle at the valley beneath them. Dark clouds loomed over the horizon. He took a swig from his bottle. "We should probably keep moving, though. Try and beat the rain."

The older brother turned back to James, who was wincing as he poured some water over his feet. He drew in his lips and dropped his pack, looking down at his brother.

"I guess this can be lunch," he said, reaching into his pack and fossicking for some food. "Wonder how Mum and Dad did climbing this."

James nodded in response.

"I like camping, but I really can't wait for a shower." The older brother offered James a cracker. "You probably can't wait to see . . . Bella," he said, smirking.

James looked down.

The older brother laughed as he drained his can of tuna onto the dirt track. He waved a fly away from the can. "Do you know what she's doing next year?"

James bit into the cracker. "I don't think she knows," he muttered, his words muffled over a mouthful of food.

The older brother sat down next to him. The faint drone of cicadas could be heard from the valley below. There were less trees now, and the sun beat down on them. The older brother put his can of tuna down.

"I know you're probably sick of Mum and Dad saying this, but you should try and suss out what you wanna do next year," said the older brother. "James?"

James didn't look up. He reached for his pack, pulled out some strapping tape and started tearing some off.

"Don't get sulky. I wish I had someone to help me with stuff like this." The older brother took another swig of water as he stood up. "James?" The older brother looked down at James, who carefully placed tape on one of his blisters. "James?"

"Can you chill?" James said, now inspecting the other foot.

The older brother shook his head and spat some water into the dirt. "We should really get going."

James shrugged, brushing a fly away from his face, and squinted at his feet.

"Your blisters are only gonna get worse in the rain . . . just . . . think for yourself." The older brother picked up his pack, grunting under the load. "Let's go."

James scrunched up some tape and looked up. "Look, if you wanna go, go – okay?" he said.

The older brother took in a breath and shook his head. He took a few steps and turned to see James still sitting there, gazing into the distance. He took a few more steps, turned one last time, then continued up the trail.

And the clouds kept moving in from the distance.

*   *   *   *   *

"I'm sure he'll be here soon. He knew where we were going," the son said, jogging up to his father. His feet ached after the day of walking. The father continued across the grass towards the trail up ahead. The headlight cast everything in an eerie white.

The father stopped, listening out for something, and the son nearly bumped into him.

Thunder rolled across the sky, closer now, but a softer rhythmic clinking rang faintly from further up the track. The father turned up his head torch.

James emerged from the bush, holding his hand up to the light.

"James?"

"Dad?"

The father dimmed his headlight as he walked over to him.

"You okay?"

"Yeah?"

"Is the camp site here?"

The father pointed across the darkness of the clearing to where the tent was.

"What happened? Why were you so far behind?"

The father helped James take his pack off, and it dropped to the ground.

He turned to the older son as lightning flickered in the sky, faintly pulsing over the camp site, then he turned back to James, who squinted against the light.

"I just had these blisters," said James.

The father furrowed his brow.

James looked at the older brother. "It was probably a bit stupid," he said. "I guess we weren't thinking."

The air was growing more humid before the storm.

"Well . . . let's not do this again, guys."

James gave the older brother a sideways smile and set off towards the tent, the mother's head torch glowed faintly from afar.

The father bent over to pick up James' pack.

"Nah, I'll take it," the older brother said, reaching down.

The father nodded, turned off his headlamp, and followed James.

The older brother grunted as he lifted the pack onto his shoulders; the straps were damp with sweat. In the darkness, he was able to make out the mother giving James a hug.

As the older brother trundled across the grass, he felt the first droplets of rain on his skin. Lightning flickered from afar accompanied by the faint drumroll of thunder. The rain was warm, and his skin tingled in the breeze.

When he got under the tarp, he dropped the pack and stared out into the rain. It was coming down harder now, and it was hard to hear much above the patter. The mother got up and stood beside the father on the other side of the tarp, the wind gently blowing in their faces. James stood beside him and handed the older brother a towel. Thunder began to crash down, and lightning flickered, bringing moments of dreamlike daylight.

They stood entranced, staring at the deluge coming down before them. Staring at the storm opening up.

Letting go of what had been held in for so long.

THERE'S A STORM BREWING

JIM KENT

"There's a storm brewing," Case remarked. A man of few words, he was.

Macca scratched his beard, studying the line of dirty, grey-black clouds hugging the horizon. "Nah," he said. "Not from that direction. Blow away to the east, it will."

Case shrugged. "Barometer's down," he said, nodding to the battered instrument hanging on the cabin wall.

"Busted," said Macca. "Ain't worked proper since Skinny Flint knocked it down." Skinny was his occasional deckhand. "Should have thrown the bloody thing overboard – Skinny too."

As the fishing boat, *Wilma K*, laboured out of the river mouth and into a slight sou'-easterly swell, Case shrugged and began to coil the rope Macca had dropped carelessly onto the deck. Always on the edge, he thought, Macca was – walking that thin line between common sense and stupidity. He only believed what he wanted to believe, and no one, from meteorologists to marine scientists, could tell him anything about the weather or the sea. If the world was flat, he would only believe it when he sailed over the edge. And the *Wilma K*? The only time the engine was serviced was when it broke down, and he couldn't remember the last time the boat had been on the slip. On the edge, he thought again, on the bloody edge, and one of these days, he'd come unstuck.

Case hoped that he wasn't on board when it happened!

"Sea's spewing over the reef," he muttered, nodding towards the swirl of white water highlighting the reef on the sea side of the lighthouse. "There has to be a bit of breeze behind it," said Case.

"Nah," Macca disagreed. "Tide's going out – always roughens up on the ebb."

Case half-expected Macca to take a short cut across the corner of the reef – he often did – but instead, he steered the *Wilma K* out around the channel buoy and well seaward of the breaking water. Once beyond the south-east corner of the reef, he angled the crayboat shoreward again, towards the line of broken rocks that formed something of a barrier between the southern bays and the ocean swells.

The *Wilma K* rocked and swayed through its slow passage into the near shore wash. Case felt the chilly tingle of salt spray on his face. He wondered if the swell was increasing. He looked seawards towards the distant horizon. The cloud didn't appear to be rising. Perhaps Macca was right – it would drift away to the east. The swell hadn't increased, he decided. The ebbing tide and the backwash from the rocky shoreline were surely responsible for the inshore agitation and the scudding spray.

Case grinned quietly to himself as he removed the long-handled gaff from its cabin wall bracket, recalling the two locals they had taken out fishing the previous week, when the sea was almost as bumpy as it was today. Their passengers had lost interest in fishing and fed a lot of berley from seasick stomachs into the sea!

"Comin' up!" Macca bellowed from the cabin. "Don't miss the bugger." He always said that, Case thought sourly, yet Case never missed gaffing a pot marker, and Macca knew it.

Case was already aware of the two bobbing white balls, indicating the position of their first craypot, and leaned over the gunwale, the point of the gaff slicing the water towards the markers. Despite the erratic effect of the sea on the boat, he easily hooked the rope beneath the markers and expertly swung it aboard and into the winch wheel. As the whirring winch hauled the craypot towards the surface, Macca turned the *Wilma K* abaft the swell, with the engine providing just enough drive to keep them from drifting back onto the rocks.

"Let's hope for a better catch than yesterday," Macca bellowed as the pot came aboard and he disengaged the winch.

One undersized crayfish and a small, slimy parrot fish!

Disgusted, Case flung the catch overboard and looked enquiringly at his skipper.

"Bait it up and put it back," Macca growled.

They hadn't taken a decent cray from the water off the south side for weeks, Case thought. They were too close to shore and bloody amateur spearfishermen!

Macca was on the edge again, refusing to believe the obvious, and positive that it would be "better" tomorrow.

Tomorrow never comes, Case thought distantly as he re-baited the pot and dumped it overboard, the markers disappearing beneath the water momentarily before bobbing back to the surface.

Macca was already urging the *Wilma K* towards the next pot marker.

Their pot line straggled along the coast from the south of the lighthouse to beyond the tip of Craggy Point. There were twenty-seven pots in all – the *Wilma K* was licensed for thirty, but they had lost three, and Macca never bothered to replace them. They had a total of three legally sized crayfish.

"Three bloody fish," Macca muttered in disgust. "One to pay for the fuel, one to keep the bank manager happy, and one for the wharf fees. Reckon we'd better get a few trumps on the way home to keep the wolf from the door."

They occasionally fished the inshore water for sweep, or trump, as they were known locally, which Macca sold at the local hotel.

"Watch for them boils off Craggy," said Macca as he turned the *Wilma K* towards the lighthouse.

"Boils" were formed by the upwards and outwards surge of water, created by the effects of the tide and currents on large inshore underwater rock formations that rose from the sea floor to near the surface. Sweep congregated close to the boils.

"Holy sh—!" shouted the usually taciturn Case.

Then Macca swore much more volubly himself, pushing the engine to full throttle and turning the bow away from the shore.

What was a lingering line of apparently dissipating cloud along the distant horizon a few minutes earlier was suddenly a swirling mass of lightning-filled madness that surged – exploded – out of the south-east and slammed into them.

Never in all of his years as a fisherman had he seen a sea rise so quickly. One moment, it was calm, a slight swell but nothing to be concerned about, and within minutes, it became a fury of towering wind-swept waves that slammed unmercifully into and over the *Wilma K*. The sea broke over the bow and starboard side of the boat, threatening to swamp them, driven to a frenzy by the wind that appeared to come from all directions at once.

Macca fought to drive his boat seaward, away from the now dangerously threatening shore. The dinghy they towed behind them was swamped and sank, holding back the *Wilma K*'s forward thrust until Case managed to reach the stern from the lee side of the cabin and cut free the connecting rope. He had barely regained the cabin before a huge wave shattered the starboard-side windows and carried away the radio aerial and life raft.

They managed to scrape around the inshore rocks, edging seaward.

"All we have to do is keep far enough offshore until we round the lighthouse reef," Macca shouted, struggling desperately to keep the swinging bow pointed towards the sea side of the distant lighthouse.

Just as long as the bloody rudder holds, Case thought, remembering again how long it had been since the *Wilma K* was on the slip.

It wasn't a broken rudder, though, that caused concern, but the forcefully determined sea that slammed without respite into their starboard, crushing the boat slowly shoreward, despite the engine at full throttle and Macca's desperate efforts to counter the threat.

The storm, with its continuous thunder and lightning and tumultuous seas, continued to rage, unabated, clinging to them as though it was already claiming ownership of the *Wilma K*.

"Gawd," Macca muttered once, struggling to keep his balance, "I reckon I know why them old sailing ship skippers hated this coast …" After all, it was known as the Shipwreck Coast. Was the *Wilma K* fated to become another rotting wreck in the rock-strewn depths?

For an hour, they struggled against the storm and the ocean until the lighthouse was close, slightly off their port bow. But they were into the inshore break, and Case realised that they would not clear the point of the reef and its waiting surf-embroiled fangs of rock.

There were two life jackets on a peg on the cabin wall, and Case eyed them doubtfully. As with a lot of other things on the *Wilma K*, they weren't in good condition, lacking care and regular attention. They might not be sturdy enough to ensure their survival when the *Wilma K* grounded. He looked at the fifty-litre drum of petrol tied to the port-side rail, just outside the cabin – Macca's contingency supply. Case decided the drum might replace the life raft, which swept overboard earlier.

He forced his way out of the cabin and managed to unleash the drum from the rail. He uncapped it and tipped it onto its side, letting the petrol pour across the deck and spray into the sea. Case knew Macca was watching him, and that, if they made it, the skipper would deduct the cost of the petrol from his wages, but he didn't give a damn. He dragged the drum into the cabin and, still ignoring Macca, secured a rope sling around it.

They were close to the reef now, floundering along its outer edge, Macca continued in his struggle to force the *Wilma K* seaward far enough to scrape around the danger and into the calmer water between the northern edge of the reef and the river mouth, where the bulk of the lighthouse promontory would provide some protection against the raging gale.

"We ain't gonna make it," Macca admitted grimly, reaching for a life jacket. "And she'll bust wide open when she hits them rocks. It's into the sea, old son."

Case, already wearing a life jacket, shoved the cabin door open and pushed the drum on to the deck. "Stick with me and hang onto the rope. The drum'll get us over the reef." *Perhaps?* A chilling thought.

They didn't see the unusually large wave bearing down onto them. A tsunami almost. The huge wave broke before it reached the *Wilma K*, and a combination of wind and backwash turned it into a fast-moving surge, a thundering maelstrom of broken water and froth. It should have smashed the *Wilma K* onto the reef and into splinters. Instead, it crashed under the boat, spinning it around and upwards, virtually hurling it across the reef and into the deeper water on the other side of the threatening outcrop. The engine, probably drowned, spluttered to a stop. Powerless, the *Wilma K* was victim to the surging water that swept it into the bay beyond the reef, the boat rocking so erratically that Case was sure that they would broach, particularly when the port side of the boat dipped briefly beneath the swell.

The storm turned away from them as quickly as it had come, as though admitting defeat, and blundered towards the distant horizon. A large swell remained but swept side-on to the shore and outside of the bay in which they found themselves. The *Wilma K*'s erratic behaviour became a slow drift towards the river mouth. Overhead, the clouds parted, and the sun broke through in splinters of light.

Macca leaned against the cabin wall and breathed deeply; his face was drained of colour.

"Bloody hell!" he murmured, almost to himself.

Case grunted. "Told you there was a storm brewing," he said.

STORMY STRANGERS

NANDI-LI O'SULLIVAN

War struck the little town. It was as relentless as a storm and just as indifferent to its occupants too. Man-made lightning reigned over the skies, illuminating empty people, who, like ocean shells, cried for their homes that were no longer with them. The sound of the soldiers was different; a steady thrum as they marched through the streets.

At the outskirts, they met a single man, clearly the last of his family; he wore the clothes of someone who worked tirelessly to provide for people besides himself. A rather ugly, green toy bunny hung from a work belt at his waist. Sobs were ripping through him; serrated pain that tore his throat and heart. The soldiers kept marching, insouciant. The man was one of many. But he didn't let the soldiers pass, and spoke in another tongue, with clear indignance, seeming to curse them. It didn't take long for the soldiers to surround and incapacitate him.

Lying there, cradled by the earth, the man felt rain like kisses on his skin and torn clothes. He wasn't sure if he kissed his kids goodbye yesterday before going to work. It felt like they were embracing him now though. The rain continued to encircle him, pitter-pattering ever so softly. A lullaby played: the tender rain and rumbling thunder. He clutched at the dampening dirt beneath him.

Soon the wind began to pick up. His hair, heavy with sweat and rain, undulated slightly, and his ears could no longer hear the soft raindrops. The sound was replaced by a rising, rushing roar. Suddenly, real hands replaced the ghostly. They were neither harsh nor uncaring, but the man was not ready to get up; he wanted to drown in his sadness. He tried to push them away, but he was picked up, nonetheless, and being held so tightly was stopping him from falling. Forced into such a position, he couldn't help but stop and reflect. On one hand, random men had blasted into the village, devastating the town and its inhabitants. On the other hand, here was someone who had never met him before but saw him and understood that he was flailing against the roiling waves of pain and loss and who was trying their best to buoy him up.

He felt confused by how these strangers could be so different. How anyone who stopped him on the street had such potential to change his life in irrevocable ways? What kind of storms would the people he meets be? Would they be like the soldiers? Crashing, wrecking, ravaging, irreverent and harsh, perennially ruinous as they made their way through life. Or would they be like the person before him? Gentle and nurturing like rain, like the wind, billowing between a soft caress to an empowering push. What kind of stranger did he want to be? The idea of what he could be for others would have to wait a while, until after he recovered, if that was possible. As he felt the steady arms around him, he thought that maybe it was. As long as there were people in this world who cared, he truly believed that there was a chance.

4

ANIMALS & STORMS

GINDLE'S SPIRIT

JADE DICKINSON

The grass waved in the breeze, swirling delicately around Gindle's feet. Though in truth, he was not real, the sounds and picturesque images brought back lost parts of him.

Sure, being a spirit was lonely, and perhaps very disheartening at times, but once you lived with it long enough, it became part of your daily routine.

Spirits are not "ghosts", as one would call them, although some do stay trapped near their resting place. Perhaps they did haunt, but it wasn't like anything living could see them anyway.

Gindle paused by a fast-flowing river, gazing deep into its darkest whirls. Oh, how he longed to dip his paw in and feel the bitter coldness of the water for at least a second. To feel how it felt to live again, that's what he wished for.

Spirits took the shape of the creature they were just before they died. If they happened to be in a fight, when dead, they would assume their shape with all their scars and wounds. And sometimes, it could bring the pain back. Sometimes, even in the afterlife, they'd have to live with sorrow, and sometimes, it was there to stay.

That's not what Gindle had though. He didn't have sadness; he had pain. Deep pain that brought desperate longing back to him. It was almost like he was haunting himself, and every time he thought of all he'd lost, another cut sliced into his heart.

He felt colder every day, knowing that creatures and nature and everything earth was made from were living on without him. But it wasn't just him. Gindle knew there were many other spirits who came from the dead. But he was different. He had no memories, not a single one. Sometimes being a spirit was worse than being turned to nothing or having no existence. Perhaps not existing would have been better than the crumbling feeling he woke to every day.

His face came into focus amongst the ripples and churning water, only a glimmer of a shape. He couldn't even remember what he was or who he was. Life was gone now, and with every passing minute, he slipped deeper and deeper into the pain that ruled his mind.

He turned away from his reflection and nearly ran headfirst into a nearby oak tree, its long, splintery branches reaching for the sky like eerie fingers. Of course, if he had bumped into it, his spirit would go right through it. Nothing could hurt him, but worst of all, nothing could touch him.

How long had it been now? Three or four years? Or more?

Gindle gave the stream one last wistful look, then turned and padded quietly through the grass, into the forest. The plants under his paws went right through him, but he was used to it now. His presence passed unnoticed, as it always did.

He trotted wearily into a large circle of pine trees, the favoured spot in which spirits gathered. Today, the space was tightly packed, as it was every day, spirits having conversations with each other like ordinary beings.

He felt a stab of pain as they hurriedly made themselves busy at the sight of him. No one knew why he didn't have any memories of his past life, but they knew it wasn't normal. They didn't want to "mingle" with the spirit that had no hope. They were perfect themselves; there was no need to think about others who might be different.

Gindle trudged over to the large silver maple situated in the centre of the grove. Many of the others had seated themselves either under the towering branches and canopy, enjoying the blissful shade, or amongst the firm offshoots.

Gindle found a shaded patch under the tree and curled up there, resting his snout on his paws.

A sudden booming voice called over the racket, startling him, and they all simultaneously turned their heads towards a large pine tree. Perched on top of it was the shimmering outline of an eagle's spirit, its sharp eyes raking the crowd like knives.

"I have a message from Yasmak!" he exclaimed, spreading his tattered wings like trophies. "The wind has humbly chosen me to remind you all The Blizzard is coming tomorrow."

A murmur of excited voices rose like a swarm of bees.

Gindle had heard of The Blizzard, but he had no idea what it might be. He noticed a couple of spirits turn to watch him, perhaps waiting for a response, which was puzzling. A small sparrow with a missing eye glanced at him, then flew up to the eagle and whispered something in his ear.

The eagle tilted his head. "May I remind you, fellow spirits, that you cannot take part in The Blizzard if you do not have a full heart – as I have heard, some of you do not." His rippling gaze passed briefly over Gindle.

Ice gripped Gindle's soul, chilling him from inside. Memories were considered a part of a spirit's heart. Whatever The Blizzard was, Gindle wouldn't be able to go unless he found his memories before it came.

"For those who don't know," the messenger went on, "The Blizzard is a great snowstorm that comes by every ten years. If you have a complete heart, Yasmak, also known as the wind, transports your soul to the stars, and you can get a second chance at life, or if you've already had that chance, your soul stays with the stars." He spread his wings again and bowed deeply. "I wish you all good luck." And with that, he leapt off the branch and flew off with a dramatic sweep of his wings.

A hush spread over the crowd, then abruptly vanished as they all burst into deafening chat and loud whispers. Everyone seemed to be excited about The Blizzard, especially those who had waited ten whole years.

Gindle lay on his side, watching a living beetle slowly make its way across a silver rock. He could see the grass through his transparent body, not flattened by his weight but standing upright as though not a thing had touched it.

A second chance at life? What if he had already gotten it?

The sun was low in the sky, bringing dusk's eerie glow. Sunset had already passed, and the light had started to disappear, vanishing behind the snow-topped mountains. It was nearly the end of winter, but to Gindle, the cold seemed to last forever.

Most spirits were starting to leave now, going back to their resting place or perhaps a favoured sleeping area.

Gindle couldn't remember his resting place. He had thought that maybe he would still have a connection, but apparently there was nothing left for him. He had searched everywhere, apart from the human encampments. He didn't like humans – they seemed cruel and terrifying.

By the time the light was fully gone, no one was left in the grove but him. He was all alone, as always.

Muffled voices woke Gindle just as the sun had left the bottom of the sky, beginning its journey to the other side. Many spirits were already wide awake, their faces full of excitement. The words "The Blizzard" seemed to be repeated a thousand times, running a continuous circle in Gindle's mind. He was still lying in the same spot he had been in the night before, underneath the silver maple in the centre of the grove. A jolly family of living birds sung their daily songs to the sky, welcoming the coming of another day.

The mountains were shrouded in a white mist, almost invisible amongst the clouds.

Other spirits were also glancing at the peaks, their eyes eager and restless. Another chance at life was probably what most of them dreamed of. Gindle knew it was true for himself.

Perhaps he should just go. Even if Yasmak didn't approve, at least he could say he tried.

By nightfall, spirits were already heading up to the mountains, and those who were more timid weren't far behind.

Gindle got to his feet and trailed hesitantly at the back of the group, feeling uncomfortable. The stars twinkled amongst the jet-black of night, like diamonds, showering them in hope.

The ground had turned to snow and rocks as they neared the top of the mountains, and the dense clouds formed a personal bubble around each of the spirits. The wind was exceptionally strong, threatening to blow them off the rickety path.

Someone up ahead gasped, and all the spirits abruptly quickened their pace.

Gindle bounded up the slope, spurred on by the thought that he was getting close, and went straight through the crowd at the top, catching himself before he tumbled over the other side of the cliff.

The spirits were waiting, watching the clouded sky for any movements, when suddenly, there was a long howl, and a gust of wind swept through them.

Gindle froze, petrified in surprise. He could *feel* the wind! It swept through him, twirling through his mind like a cleanser and washing away his unhappiness with it.

All the others seemed to feel it too, matching pictures of enjoyment painted across their faces.

Snow began to pelt down on them, taking part in the layers that covered the ground like a giant duvet. Gindle lifted his snout up to the night sky, his eyes shining. Nothing had ever ignited this feeling of delightfulness inside him.

There was a sudden silence.

He turned to see the other spirits staring at the centre of The Blizzard, their transparent bodies quivering.

Something was moving in the midst of the spirits, a swirling tendril, diving and dipping in the storm. It paused for a minute, its glowing snake-like eyes studying them like new-found jewels. They stilled on Gindle, who wondered if he was imagining the expression of pity that passed its face. For a long moment, it just stared at him, then tossed its head and transformed into a horse, lifting its long neck to the sky with a snort of excitement. Yasmak.

The gale grew stronger, then started to morph together, creating a tornado of snow, wind and spirits. Gindle watched as the spirits obligingly let Yasmak sweep them into the whirlwind. He glanced sadly down at his paws, knowing no tendril would lift him up. He was just a lost little spirit with no memories and no life.

It seemed like years until the winds died down and the tornado vanished into a snowfall. Gindle watched each snowflake as it fell and slowly drifted to the floor below. Oh, how he wished he could touch them.

Then suddenly, the horse appeared. Its mane was a rippling mass of wind, blowing gently in the breeze it had created. Its eyes had the same pitiful look they had before.

"You don't know," Yasmak said gently, whipping its tail like a trapped snake. "I thought you knew."

"What?" Gindle managed to say, lowering himself into a respectful bow. "What don't I know?"

The horse regarded him for a long moment. "I know who killed you," it said sadly.

Gindle blinked at Yasmak. He wasn't sure if he even wanted to know this. What good would it do him now? He felt suddenly more hollow and dead than ever.

"Humans are creatures of disaster," the horse continued. "They kill helpless animals just to make themselves feel safer. They killed you – I am sorry."

Gindle bared his teeth. "That still doesn't answer why I can't remember anything! Who am I?"

Yasmak raised its head to the hailstones raining down from the raging storm above. The horse stamped its hoof once, and suddenly, the land of snow, trees, and rocks vanished, and they were surrounded by a whirlwind of memories.

Gindle was frozen in fright, and his heart itself seemed to be leaking tears.

In front of him was himself, pacing in a small, wired space, every now and again lifting his head up to sniff the air. And for the first time in years, Gindle got a glimpse of what he was. His ears were rounded at the top, similar to a bear's. His body was like a dog's, slim and smooth, and he had a strip of long stripes from the middle of his back down to his black, skinny tail. A thylacine. The creature stared dejectedly out of the bars for a long moment, then the memory started to fade away, and another took its place.

Gindle winced, wanting to look away. The bloodstained body of a thylacine was strung across a wooden table, and the triumphant human stood next to it, brandishing their kill like a trophy. The picture melted away and went back to Gindle's old self again. This time, he was lying down on the barren ground. A couple of humans outside the cage were banging the fence, trying to get his attention, but he was too worn out, lonely, sad and caged up to move. He was dying. The flame that had been lit in his heart from when he was born was melting away like ice. His onlookers waited for a response, their faces full of boredom, and then suddenly, his eyes closed and his body stilled, and the memory faded abruptly to black.

Yasmak stood clearly in front of Gindle; its eyes were full of sympathy. "I hope you can remember now," it said, bowing its head to him. "They took your pelt, and your memories along with it."

Gindle looked away, not wanting to think about what had happened. "Is there any way I can get another life?"

"I'm sorry," Yasmak whispered gently. "But your tribe died off long ago. They're long gone – you were the last of them. The stars can't give you another chance . . . you don't exist anymore."

Gindle felt as if his heart was ripped open. His tribe had been hunted to extinction, and the humans had kept him – the last thylacine – in captivity. There really was no point to stay alive anymore, even as a spirit.

"But," the horse said, "there's somewhere you can be."

There was a shift in the air, and suddenly, many shapes appeared in front of him. They were striped and had elegant snouts. They stared, blinking at their last friend ever to come from the living world. Gindle stared back.

"All your fellow tribemates have been waiting." Yasmak tilted its head. "I took them with me. Where else would they have to go? Will you come, Gindle?"

Gindle nodded, feeling hesitant yet happy.

Memories were still playing over in his head, telling him of the pain he had suffered. But that was over. Now he was living in a spirit world where pain was gone but memories still survived. And even though life sometimes wasn't what you wanted it to be, you could always find a way to live when surrounded by beings who understood what you had been through.

STORM FLIGHT

MIEKE HEYKOOP

The wind howled between rock faces and across the sheltered eyrie, gaining strength and slashing the dark sea below into choppy white-capped waves. Skor shivered in his nest next to his brother and sister. He looked up at Father's and Mother's windswept golden forms as they lashed their tails and whispered at the entrance.

"Are you sure?" Mother was asking, her voice so soft that Skor could scarcely hear her. "None of them are exceptional yet, but Skor is just so terrible at storm flying."

"The sky is black as far as the eye sees. Only the lightning breaks it up. If we linger, it may get worse and trap us here. We must make a decision now."

Skor didn't know if he wanted to hear their decision. Would they wait? Go? Gryphons always migrated just ahead of the storm season, but it looked like his first migration would happen in the middle of a storm.

And Mother was absolutely right about Skor. He squeezed his eyes closed, memories of Father's lessons flashing to mind. Bruises. Constant rescues. Laughter. It still stung. *I'll never be good at storm flying.*

But he couldn't stay here by himself through winter. If they left, Father would show him the way . . . and maybe if Skor imitated him exactly, he could do it. His brother, Rak, huffed next to him and fluffed his feathers. Faur, their sister, just whimpered.

"Should we wait it out, then?" Mother asked, casting a golden eye at the eyrie's exit.

"The storm season is abreast of us now," Father growled. "We either race the storm, or we stay here for winter."

"We'd starve!"

"Then we must go. I'll rouse the chicks."

Skor hastily shut his eyes, breathing hard as Father's talons clicked on the stone floor.

His warm beak nudged Skor. "Bestir yourselves," he said, his voice softer and his crest rising and falling. He shoved Rak gently with a talon towards the edge of the nest. "We're flying at once. The migration is beginning now, and you must be awake. Quickly, now, my children!"

Skor trembled, looking up at the blanketed black sky, so bleak, colourless and *threatening*. They couldn't possibly outrun that. It was all around them, growling and flashing. It would tear off their wings, throw them into the sea . . .

"Come along, stay near me or your father, and we'll get on," Mother assured each chick, ruffling feathers and fur with her beak. "Don't get split up. The wind is strong, but you were all taught to fly through a storm. You'll be fine as long as we stay close."

"What if we get separated?" Skor asked. His feathers bristled against his will.

"We won't. You know the way. I've shown you from the sky before."

Mother was *fighting* to sound reassuring. She mustn't have noticed the fear lashing in her tail or rippling in her smaller crest.

But they were already perched on the edge of the eyrie. Skor tasted his fear and bile, his heart beating against his rib cage.

"Do not fight the wind unless you must. Go with it as you can," Father said. And Skor could have sworn the words were aimed at him.

And Father leaped into the sky with a powerful thrust of his hind legs. The wind tossed him about like a dried leaf, but he stabilized and charted a clean-cut line towards the distant midway island. Sometimes he flapped, and sometimes he trimmed his wings and let the wind go past him.

Imitate him. But how?

Rak leaped next, encouraged by Mother. Then she nudged Skor, and he leaped.

And his world pitched. Wind tore at his wings and snatched the breath from his lungs. It howled in his ears and threw him sidelong. His beak parted, and he gasped, translucent eyelids covering his eyes from the worst of the gale. Dimly, he saw Father's figure flying ahead and pressed to follow, already panting.

How could he get through this? Already, his breath had lagged, and his wings screamed as though he'd flown for hours.

"Do not fight the wind unless you must. Go with it as you can."

Skor felt the wind. It fought him, pushing and pulling and stealing his breath, even as he tried to imitate Father's pattern of flapping, and trimming, and soaring and finding his currents. Why wasn't it working? Spread his wings right now? No! He flailed, overcorrecting and squawking in terror as he swept sideways. One minute, he saw the sea, then the angry sky, then finally righted himself and looked towards the horizon.

Up ahead – was that a wall of *rain* coming towards him?

And Father had gone straight on, leaving Skor well behind even his siblings. Skor tilted his wings and caught the wind for a moment, sailing in the wake of his siblings, and then—

Rain. Water got up his nose and into his beak. It blurred his sight and made it impossible to see Father or Mother or his brother and sister. Water soaked through his feathers and fur, weighing down his wings until it felt as though stone blocks were fastened to his feathers, faltering against his efforts to flap harder.

Glide. Ride wind currents, stall against the wind until it dies back. How many times had Mother said that? He could almost hear her voice now. *But what did that mean?!*

His wings wouldn't level. He pitched from one side to the other, flaring and flapping and rolling. A gust slashed him across the face, then swept behind him and pushed him forward.

It threw him into a tailspin. Where was Father? Where was Mother, or Rak, or even Faur? He couldn't see them. Had he gone too far off course? And worse, exhaustion burned through his wings, and it took all his willpower to keep flapping.

If he stopped flying, he'd fall into the water. He had to make it to the midway point . . . if the rain would stop getting in his eyes!

A second gust cut, stinging drops across his face, but this time, he was ready. He spread his wings and caught the return draft, sweeping forward on billowing wings.

Everything was wet. Windy. Cold. Oh, he could feel the water seeping all the way through his feathers and into the fur of his hindquarters.

Where's Father? Where's Mother? He let out a shriek, but the wind swallowed it.

The first cold edges of panic touched his racing heart.

What should he do? Keep going? But what if he was heading out to sea instead of charting a course towards the midway island? Would Father come looking for him if he stayed in one place, or would that take too long?

A whimper slipped out of him, and he swallowed it back. If the rain would just *stop,* he could see where he was going and touch down somewhere, then wait for Father.

But as far as he knew, the only island on his way was the one at the halfway point. And in this storm, he couldn't see where it was.

How long had he even been out here? It felt like hours and minutes all at once.

Keep going, he told himself, zigzagging through slashing rain in search of aother gust he could ride. Stopping wasn't an option. *I can't do this. I can't do this—*

Exhausted wings flared to catch another gust. *Oh! Ow!* A shriek escaped him as a powerful blow snapped his wings all the way open, nearly ripping the appendages from their sockets.

The speed pitched him headlong, and he tumbled, skimming the whitecaps with his claws. Wings faltered. *No, no, no!* Talons brushed the waves.

Skor heaved, muscles burning, and flapped skyward. Feathers skimmed the waves, and for a terrible moment, Skor saw himself sinking and drowning in the water. *No!*

A final, titanic heave, and he was up, flapping like a fledgling just getting his wings under him for the first time and fighting the headwind.

Up ahead, he glimpsed something in the rain. An island? A jutting rock? Skor tried to aim for it, but his zigzagged path made aiming nigh impossible and he could hardly *see!*

Talons outstretched. Another gust threw him sidelong, and then came back, whipping up through his wings and throwing him violently against the jutting island below. All the breath drove from his lungs, and shivering, wings aching, Skor hauled himself into the shadow of the rock, cutting back some of the rain.

He sniffled. *Now what? Was this the midway island? If so, where were Mother and Father?*

A cautious thrust of his head granted him a view outside, but with the slashing rain, he couldn't see far enough to tell where he was.

Rest. Wait for the rain to stop. Then figure out where I am and move, Skor told himself.

There was nothing else to do, and he had the inkling that this wasn't the midway island. Too small, for one thing, and too rocky.

He'd figure something out. Surely, he couldn't have gone *that* far off course.

But Skor watched the sky and chirruped worriedly to himself, because maybe he had.

Night was just descending when the rain stopped. The wind howled, gusting over the rocks and ruffling damp feathers and fur. Skor hauled himself to the edge of the rocks and looked out, turning his head from side to side.

Water lapped at his claws. *What?* His gaze dropped in astonishment. Hadn't the water been lower?

The tide! Skor realized in panic. If he stayed here, the rock would be entirely covered!

He scrambled higher onto the rocks and looked out, but there were no other islands in sight. The shore of the migratory mainland was not in sight, and he couldn't even see the eyrie.

Oh no. Skor shrank in on himself. He had no idea which direction to go, and the wind was still strong. Keen eyes scanned the angry sky but could find no trace of parents or siblings.

Did I go past it? Skor wondered. He paced in front of the shallow cave. Already, the winds were changing from the warm summer he'd grown up with. Soon it would get cold.

He couldn't stay here. The water was still rising. He had to leave.

What had Mother and Father said about situations like this? *Find the north star,* Father had often said. But he couldn't see the stars for the clouds. *The sun sets in the west and rises in the east. The mainland is north, and the island is too.*

It all meant nothing! How did he know if he'd gone past it, or if it was directly to his side, or what?

Go to a high place. Father had said that, too, hadn't he?

Skor climbed to the highest point on the island and filled his lungs, then lunged off the rocks into the air. The ache spread in his wings again, but the wind wasn't as strong, and he glided on currents, climbing higher and higher until he could see a great distance around him.

And way off in the distance ahead of him, he saw the smear of a jagged island and a tree.

That's it!

And it meant he'd made a pittance of progress. Mother and Father must be worried sick ... if they hadn't already gone on without him. *If they made it.*

Night was falling, but if he waited for Father, his little island would be submerged. Did he have the strength to make it to the island? If the storm wasn't over ... and the sky suggested it was not ...

Skor glided in a wide circle. *Go,* he told himself. *Look how black the sky is! Look how high the water is! Don't wait for it to get worse!*

But what if I go and the storm rises again?

And what if it doesn't?

I still can't fly in a storm. I don't know how!

He growled and shook his head. Deep breaths. Then he angled towards the island and trimmed his wings for a swift flight.

The wind immediately rose in his face, and he fought it for a useless moment, then gasped.

Oh, of course! He envisioned Father trimming his wings and flying as the wind pulled back. Father hadn't been *performing* a set of motions, he'd been *reacting* to the wind! That was why it had never worked for Skor.

And for the first time, he *understood* what he was supposed to do.

The wind rose again, but this time, he angled his wings to reject it, pulling them as close as he dared and simply holding his position as it pushed against him. When it died back, he pushed forward, flying much easier.

It shoved and pushed at him, but he had some idea how to fly with it now, and trimmed his wings, plunging and climbing at serrated intervals. *I can do this.*

He had to get there before his family moved on. If they hadn't already.

His wings screamed at him, burning his chest with each ragged breath. And the rain stirred again.

Despair ran cold through his blood. If he lost sight of that island, he'd never find it again!

But he pressed on, dredging up every ounce of strength and pushing his way through the storm.

Almost there!

His beak parted, sucking in air, tongue lolling and throat burning. *Don't give up!*

If he fell in the water, he would die. Gryphons were terrible at swimming, and the choppy water below might well have been the jaws of a beast.

Focus!

Brown flecked wings beat harder, and he strained forward, front talons curling and releasing.

And suddenly, he saw it. Spread below him, the island looked like a paradise.

Skor winged down, chirping and shrilling in hopes of attracting attention. He struggled to lose altitude. Wind kept filling his wings and pushing him back up, so he trimmed and trimmed until he was plummeting at an alarming rate. He slowly nudged out more and more wing until he pulled up and landed hard on the rock.

For a moment, he didn't move. Scarcely breathed.

I made it, he told himself, hauling himself upright. *I made it! And now I know how to fly in a storm!*

And he called out, a cry somewhere between a shriek and a roar.

Then he listened, pricking tufted ears and straining his neck to its full length. He called out again, straining his ears.

An answering cry rode on the breeze, and he went rigid, unsure if it was his own cry echoing back to him. *Please be my mother, please,* he thought, advancing at a nervous pace. He called again.

And then the cry came, shriller this time, and a golden figure appeared on the rise. Tension fled his body, and he crumpled down in a boneless heap.

I did it! I caught up!

UNDER A WILD FULL MOON

BROOKS CARVER

Snow fell on north-eastern Tennessee that Christmas Day of 1858, with a seriousness never before seen by inhabitants living in those parts. It fell as if to cover all of nature's work, utterly and convincingly, forever. That morning, when John and Jennie left church services, instead of walking home, they received a ride in the wagon of Maynard and Jo Watkins, who dropped them off where the path to their cabin wound along the creek branch.

"Why don't you come on over to our house?" Maynard said. "We're going to worry about you in all this weather."

"We need to get on home. It's not going to get any better later on," John said. "Thanks for the ride."

By the time they had walked a hundred yards down the one-lane trace, the older couple in the wagon had vanished up the road into the driving whiteness. Even the tracks were obliterated.

"My goodness, Johnny, don't you let go of my hand. I'm liable to get myself lost out here. I never seen nothing like this before. Have you?"

"I've seen it this bad up on the mountain, but not down here. We'll just follow the fence line, and everything will be fine. Don't worry."

The wind freshened and began to move the snow. Stinging particles bit at their faces and hands. John directed Jennie off the trace to the fencerow, and they struggled along, pulling themselves by the toprails. The snow swept in, thick, blinding, and heavy, pushed by an ever-increasing blast of wind. It turned that hour into a full-fledged blizzard, a whirling, building chaos of white. Staggering from the savage freezing wind, John's nearly frozen hands found his wife.

"Come on, darling," he shouted. Jennie didn't answer. He pulled her along behind him in the general direction of the cabin. She fell, and he picked her up in his arms and staggered forward, crashing blindly onto the porch. He opened the door, and they staggered, exhausted and freezing, to the floor. He kicked the door shut and scrambled to the fireplace, plunging his hands into the ashes. John prayed aloud for hot coals. His hands were slightly burned while stirring the fire into life.

While John was feeding the blaze, Jennie lit a taper. She put the candle on the mantel and warmed her hands over the tiny flame. "That there was the coldest I ever been in my whole life, Johnny." Outside, the wind whistled and moaned.

"Just give me a minute here, and I'll get some coffee started. I believe there's a skim of ice on the water barrel!" She punched at it with a hatchet.

Slowly, the tingling and needles of pain in her feet, hands, ears, and nose told Jennie that the room was warming. A circle of heat spread outward, and after a few hours, the temperature in the little cabin ticked at a slow pace above freezing.

The first savage howls came like a lamentation from some far away, unexplored place. The animals were near, in the woods behind the pasture, and called to the beauty of the winter night. The chilling sound awakened John in the first hour after midnight. He arose, put on his canvas trousers and sheepskin coat, and then struggled into his boots. The wind blustered on, shook the cabin, and seemed to mock him, but John decided to get a closer look. After closing the front door, he stood on the porch for a moment and looked out upon a land transformed and alien in the moonlight. A wolf cried out again, then another. Edging along in the shadow of the wall, John moved to the back of the cabin. By the light of the cold winter moon, he caught a glimpse of the animals as their ghostly forms, trailing a cloud of snow, moved from the edge of the timber and flowed into the valley. His heart nearly stood still.

"Oh, God, what do they want?" Jennie appeared next to him.

"Nothing from us," said John.

Wolves had never been so bold or close to civilization in his memory. They appeared to be a family, and he counted nine of them streaming into the pasture. The alpha male was in the lead as they trotted into John's view. The gray leader seemed to look John's way, then paused and sang out a slow, long moan. Then one voice after another – some deep, some high – in perfect harmony, called out to their private, uncharted, savage heaven.

"I'm scared of wolves," Jennie said. "They're not supposed to be down here, are they?"

"Don't be afraid."

"There's so many of 'em, Johnny. They might get into our cattle. *They might get us!*"

"This is a rare sight. Stay still. Don't move around so."

"Let's get back inside," Jennie whispered. "Come on now."

"Hush. Stay still."

The family of wolves ran through the powdery drifts, rolling over and chasing each other playfully, around and around. The pack then formed into a long, irregular line and then vanished with ghostly grace, like phantoms on some secret mission, back into the timber. First they were there, and then they were gone. John could barely breathe, thinking of what he had just seen. The leader from the edge of the trees sang out once more, and his song echoed through the mountain passes and down the valley.

"Can we go in now? I think they knew we were here. They might come back."

John stared across the moonlit pasture to where the pack had faded into the woods. He felt like the wolf had told him goodbye. Within minutes a fresh breeze had covered all their tracks.

"It's all right," he said. "They've gone. I doubt they'll be down here ever again."

The couple went inside, stoked up the fire, and climbed back into bed to the warmth of each other's bodies.

A DREAMING DOG #11
STARING AT AN ANIMAL'S EYES

NICHOLAS JEFFERS

Beware
The narrator
Only speaks of self

Indulging in gravity's
Undulations
In dreams

The crown

Is stripped of reality's
Invisible clothes
And goes unrecognized

You peek at the future
Until time burns it down
Along with all other possibilities

Into the now;
What is.

And then you see it
Like the silent language
Of the deaf

Understanding beyond
Sonic vibration
A perfect dance
Of material

Beyond sight,
You,
A light

5

WORLDS & FUTURES

THE BACKWARDS GOD

CL GLANZING

The arm was withered, salt-crusted, and puckered by a taught mesh of seaweed. The bicep ended abruptly in a jagged flap of translucent tissue, bristling in the sea wind.

Bloodless, our black sand clung to its thick hairs. The fingers were as dark as the waves crashing on the rocks. And, like most Andalonians, the mottled flesh flushed algae-green when you squeezed.

I extended the fingers with my own, until we were mirrored, palm to palm. The man's hand was much wider than mine, and supple, as if awakening from a nap. I interlocked our fingers, and the chill made my shoulders shiver.

No other flesh had rolled onto our black-pebbled beach after last night's storm, mashed or desiccated by the rocks in the shallows. The rest of the crescent coastline looked pristine, a monotonous colour broken only by yellowing seaweed. I did not have to continue my search to the end of the cape.

But Father would still be pleased. I tucked the arm in my string sack and ran back the way I had come. My new, wider footsteps pressed against my previous indentations.

Our cave nestled between two bluffs worn smooth by sea, wind, and rain. The tide did not reach so far inland anymore.

My eyes adjusted quickly to the gloom. Father was bent over the stone table, our new man lying outstretched before him, cloth swept over his face and groin.

Father raised his sewing arm confidently, drawing the flaps of stomach skin together with a fishbone needle, as tightly as if he were closing two lips. The cavity had been stuffed with dried kelp.

I showed Father the treasure in my strong sack.

"Good, good," he said, tousling my hair. "One is better than none."

Legs were always the priority – unless Father could fashion a sufficient stump from driftwood, but this was less than ideal.

I watched Father kneel and place the arm on a flat board on the ground. He took the serrated blade from his tool belt and began to saw the unnecessary folds of flesh, neatly tidying the end as one would slice bread. The muscle was frigid and reluctant to part, but Father was persistent.

He held the clean cut against the man's shoulder, pressing bone to bone. I saw his fingers tremble a little as he reached for needle and thread.

"Father – the wrong side," I said, looking at the way the thumb pointed away from the thigh.

"So it is," he said, and rounded the stone table to the other side. His eyesight was declining with every season. I always threaded his needles for him.

"A bit short, but it'll have to do," Father said. He pinched the flesh, drawing the emerald together with the sunrise-orange of the shoulder. Father relied on the vision provided to him by his fingertips, expertly applying the stitches to sinew, veins, and muscle.

"Bring the muck, son," he said to me. I brought the wooden barrel from the outer lip of our cave, too pungent to leave where we slept. It was heavy, and my scrawny arms hardly met across its circumference. I rocked it side to side, walking it an inch at a time.

You must dig deeply – at least the height of me – to reach the good mud, taken from the tidal pools that dry in the summer heat, crushed with salt and dried algae. A reeking slime of fishbones, ground shells, scales, lichen, seaweed.

I helped Father spoon the mixture onto our man and massaged the foul clay into his skin – arms, legs, stomach, face – then we rolled him over and continued. We wrapped strips of kelp around his body, west to east.

Father placed his hands over the mound of plant and mud covering the man's face. I joined him in the prayer to the Backwards God, our voices low and lacquered with fatigue.

Starving on a Friday, a man begs the sea for food. The next day, he vomits into the waves. On the Sunday, he catches the largest haddock that he has ever seen. Our God in reverse.

I bundled Father's mat and dragged it outside the cave to our firepit. I did not mind sleeping on the beach when the sand was warm.

Father followed me out of the cave, stooped, one hand to his lower back and his shoulders touching his ears. His white hair and beard met the grey curls on his chest. He had four good teeth left.

We sealed the mouth of the cave with a lattice of reeds and smooth branches.

I made a fire and reboiled a fish broth from yesterday. I placed a blanket over Father's knees, and he swatted me away, telling me not to fuss.

I lay on the sand across from Father. The night air was spiced with woodsmoke. Not from our fire but from the west. Burning ships.

Grey gulls shrieked and dove above the surf, which tumbled and split against the black rocks shadowed in the setting sun.

My eyes were heavy, and my head dropped onto my outstretched arm. I began to skim the surface of a dream in which I was underwater, watching pockets of air rise above my face. I wondered what it would be like to drown.

I heard footsteps and opened my eyes to the night air that had descended over our camp site. A figure approached. I had not heard the lattice move.

"Ah," said my father, warmly, cordially. He stoked the fire. "Come and join us."

The naked man approached, still coated in a fine layer of muck. Most had sloughed, along with the kelp. The bloating of his face and limbs had vanished, and his muscles were now visible under taut, but heavily scarred, skin. He swayed as he walked, the one arm stiffly at his side.

His face was curious, hapless, and a little afraid. Trying to reconcile fear with wonder. His brow, which had once been creased by years of furrowing, sat raised and open.

"Warm yourself," my father directed, offering him a clay bowl brimming with broth. The man looked at it for a moment, before wrapping the fingers of one hand around the base. He seemed surprised by his own instinct.

"Good lad," said Father, watching the man raise the bowl slowly to his lips.

"Do you remember your name?" Father asked. The man opened his mouth a fraction and then closed it. He shook his head, then stared at the abrupt ending of his left shoulder. As if trying and failing to remember what should be there.

"No matter, no matter," said Father. "Were you travelling the seas?"

"Yes," the man managed. "A ship." His eyes lifted and lightened. "A warship."

The man looked to me and then back at Father. "Are you Andalonian or Firkkner?" The syllables slurred quickly together like a song or greeting said so many times that its meaning becomes buried.

Father chuckled and shot me a glance. He taught me not to be alarmed by this question. Ideologies always linger in the mind, he said. Men are taught to value them above their own names and selves.

"Oh, we stay out of all of that," replied Father. "What do you think you are?"

The man frowned and ran his fingers over the raised, white line dividing his thigh. The scars of stitches separating green flesh from orange.

Father seemed pleased. "Do not trouble yourself with that now." He clapped the man on the back. "In the morning, we will give you a sack with enough dried fish and water jugs to last a while. You will walk down the shore for a day until you reach a delta. Follow the river inwards for another two days. There you will find a new village with people such as yourself."

The man looked out to the indigo waves, and the black rocks sparkling by our fire light. He looked to the sea as a babe would to its mother. Longing, yearning, suddenly bereft to be leaving home.

"A new life," added Father, sensing his hesitation. "Peaceful."

The man turned back to the fire and nodded dutifully at what the old man said.

In the morning, we watched the man disappear down the dark beach into the horizon, leaving footprints of two sizes. He wore a new tunic that I had woven myself from seagrasses.

"One by one," Father smiled as he trundled back into the cave. "One by one."

As always, a touch of melancholy tugged my chest, watching the man become smaller in the distance, but there was also a placid relief.

I prefer them when they were quiet on the table, I thought to myself as I absent-mindedly traced the scar running the length of my sternum.

Yes, I like it best when it's just Father and me and the Backwards God.

BATTERY LIFE

MEREDITH DOWNES

The television was the first to go. It went with the power, hissing a white-noise death and ending with a phut. Only a small dot on the screen remained. I stared at that dot and listened to the rush of blood in my ears as my world came crashing down. The sound was deafening in that new silence.

I fumbled my way across the room and passed the gaping window frame. It was dark out there, dark everywhere. My fingertips struck the smooth, hard shell of my computer and held on. I had turned it off in the hours before, even pulled the plug. Nobody knew what was going to happen. Maybe there would be surges. I wanted to protect it. Something bubbled in my throat that might have been a laugh. I had been trying to protect my computer.

Only the battery was left now – eight hours. The battery would last eight hours. My mind clung to that number. Beyond it was a void I could not envision. My index finger pushed the power-on button. The computer chimed as it booted up, black display turning to light, words across it. A subtle sense of order restored beamed out at me. I could hear, too, the faint hum of its insides whirring and imagine the current coursing through it. It was enough.

My phone hadn't rung since the morning. I'd left it on permanent redial, the noise fading into the background, the endless disconnect. I went to stop that now. There were only two hours left on the phone's battery. It would be the next to go. My hand jerked as the small screen illuminated and the ringtone pealed out. More comforting words flared up into my blinking eyes. *Answer. Reject.* Carefully, I forced my thumb to choose. A voice, echoing and scratchy, surfaced from the speaker. *Are you there? Are you there? Are you there?* Over and over, she said it.

I licked my lips, dry tongue on dry, and tried to make them move. I stared around at the shadowy room, etched in the white gleam of my laptop. Before I could speak, the phone beeped into nothing, and the voice was gone. When it rang again, there was crying on the other end – only crying this time. It didn't sound like her, but I could never know for sure.

That was the last thing my phone would do. As the minutes passed, the little bars disappeared one by one until, with a spinning wheel death throe, its light went out completely. I pushed the on/off button, the flesh blanching beneath my thumbnail. Only a memento mori battery with exclamation point appeared. I traced its outline on the screen before it too faded away. I let my phone slip from my hand and shatter on the floor.

A new sound, fists on wood, boomed through the quiet. *I saw your light. I saw the light under your door. Can I come in? Can I see where the light comes from?* I snatched my computer and huddled it down under the desk. This light was mine, this last light. I held its electronic hum to my ear and hummed along, my lips vibrating in harmony with the vibrations within. I was one with my machine, there, at the end. I waited until the noise at the door went away.

I slept then, lulled by the pulse of my computer's circuitry. Only the ping of the low battery alert could awaken me. It would not be long now. My eyes stayed fixed on the screen, and I began to shake. I dreaded the three-second automatic shutdown. When it came, it would be quick. I knew that from before. Before, when it hadn't mattered.

There was nothing my computer could do now. Nothing it could connect to. Nothing it could show. Yet, bathed in its pale glow, its droning density beneath my hands, it was still something more than the nothing that surrounded me, and I along with it.

Its death rattle would shudder through me like my own. The display blazed a fatal flash, before the blackness consumed it. My fingers worked at the keys, the buttons and switches, but not even an indicator light could I revive. The afterimage beneath my lids was all that was left me. It was all I could hold onto in that final moment. But I knew even that memory of light would soon be eclipsed.

With one last caress of warm plastic, I laid my computer down amongst the cords and other remains. I snapped the cover shut, and I opened my eyes to let the dark shine in.

THE OBSERVATION OF THINGS PAST

CONOR SCANLAN

3 SEPTEMBER 2027

An eye passed today as I worked. The wind dropped. Replacing it, a vacuum of *no-sound*, taking me all the way back to the beginning. No, not the day the lights went out, but the day Vera left, Adeleine with her. She bundled our daughter onto the bike and left without a word.

Status report. I've jury-rigged the last of the reticulated dampener pylons due south of the observatory. Food supplies remain sufficient. I am three days from the initial test phase. If only Vera could see me now, about to take us back to where we used to be, with more electricity than the settlement could ever hope to use.

My family will belong to me again.

5 SEPTEMBER 2027

The test phase will be delayed. At least a week. Pylon 17-S short-circuited overnight, and repairs will take time. I tipped over my bookcase and tore the plans from the wall, ripping their pages in satisfying handfuls. I may have injured myself. My arms have cuts and bruises. If Vera was here, she would tend to them, but she is not, and Adeleine is not, and I am alone.

These frustrations accumulate, building into something greater. The crack of perpetual thunder seems to mock me and my efforts. This storm-blasted world, sometimes it makes me want to scream. If I were a religious man, I would have gods to blame, but in this world, I can only blame myself.

Slashes of monsoon rain pattered at my window last night. The shutter came loose, shorn from its hinges. It was like the early days, before we all realised the world would never be the same. Nature was busy reasserting a primal balance and would not be denied.

How naive we had been. Every one of us.

6 SEPTEMBER 2027

A memory struck me today – Adeleine around the time of her fourth birthday. I'd come home late from work at the university to find her tucked into bed beside Vera. Thunder rumbled in the distance.

Vera stroked our daughter's forehead, flattening her fringe. The bedside light emitted a measure of warmth. Shadows danced on the wall from an animal mobile Adeleine was already too old for.

I sat beside them both, and together, we counted the seconds between bursts of thunder – seven seconds, then eight, then eleven. The greater the length of time between thunderclaps, the further away a storm would be. An elegant concept any child could understand.

Adeleine moved to my lap, and I explained the storm was growing distant, moving further away from us. We would be safe, and storms were nothing to be afraid of in any case.

Adeleine soon fell asleep in my arms, and once she had, I returned her to bed.

Why am I thinking of this now? A memory of lightning and the thunder, before it defined all our lives – before it took over everything.

11 SEPTEMBER 2027

There was an explosion in the settlement last night. I felt the vibrations, even at this altitude. The sound cut through the thunderstorm. I prised open the broken window and watched a gout of flame and fury mushroom into the night sky. Beyond it, in every direction, storms raged and engulfed the sound intruding on their domain. Spot fires flared, and an icy hand gripped my heart. *Vera and Adeleine.* For the first time in what felt like years, I yearned to leave my post, abandon everything, and seek them out.

I rejected the foolish notion. My work was more important. I may be beyond saving, but my work, when it succeeds, will change everything. To not only neutralise the lightning, but to harness its energy – its very life force – and use it to rebuild the world that the storms ended.

I drew the window closed. Unable to sleep, I write this now, knowing tomorrow the initial test phase will begin at last.

27 SEPTEMBER 2027

Delayed again. My wounds are not healing. The electrical burns that lace my forearms like coiling snakes are the most painful.

Every time the eye of the storm reaches me, an immovable dread settles inside. When I'm engaged in my work, I rarely, if ever, think of Vera and Adeleine. Thinking of them is for the night-time as I write. When the storms clear, there is no respite, only torture. When the eye hovers above me, I can't think of anything *but* them and the life we once shared. An acute self-consciousness colours my existence, and for that brief window, I can't do anything but sit and wait for it to pass.

Something feels *missing* in those moments – the bang and crash of thunder, the hammering of turbulent winds, and rainfall, battering the land. But it's something more, which emerges only in the silence of whatever is observing us.

Something is missing, and I can't let myself get distracted. Not when I'm so, so close.

Tomorrow will be the day. I promise this to myself. No matter what happens.

28 SEPTEMBER 2027

Success at last! If only Vera could see what I've accomplished. And Adeleine, too – to see her daddy in a new light. The one who ushered in a whole new world. I write now, bathing in electrically generated artificial light. Why did we ever think of this light as "artificial", disparaging the creation that once made the modern world *possible*. The reinvention – *my* reinvention – that will return us to modernity, all over again.

Adeleine will have a daddy she can be proud of. I imagine the way Vera, too, will look at me when the storms stop. Yes, it will take some time to get used to. I don't relish the thought of living within an endless *eye*. It *is* necessary, though, to rebuild what we have lost. There is no future in beginning again from nothing.

I must remain steadfast. With the initial test complete, I will run the converters first thing tomorrow and process the acquired energy into storage, ready to be fed down to the settlement.

29 SEPTEMBER 2027

The conversion proceeds apace. Today I activated the LGPC – the laser-guided plasma channel – and it was a resounding success! Attracting every lightning strike in an approximate twenty-five-kilometre radius, distributed across the observatory's twenty-one lightning rods, with a percussive consistency. The sound is ear-splitting. I sense the shift in air pressure, even from within these sturdy walls.

It is a little-respected fact that a typical thunderstorm contains enough raw power to rival a nuclear bomb. It's no wonder that a series of ceaseless thunderstorms was able to exact such a precise vengeance in such a short amount of time.

Even accounting for the drop-off of power by the time lightning reaches the ground, the energy my system harvests is phenomenal. Within a week, at an estimate, storage will reach its first gigawatt – enough to power a small city. At that stage, phase two will begin. Once I convert the high voltage to low, it will be ready for distribution.

I think with glee of the change that must already be taking place in the settlement below: the shantytown and its ignorant inhabitants, watching the observatory's peak and its permanent shroud of fierce lightning; people living in an *eye* that has already lasted approximately thirty-six and a half hours. Do they wonder aloud to each other, *Is it over?*

Of all of those simplistic minds, only Vera will understand.

Now I must go and let the turbulence rock me into a much-needed sleep.

I am content.

1 OCTOBER 2027

Vera. Adeleine. If you're reading this, then know, these past years, even though it led to *this*, both of you were the only good things to ever happen to me. I didn't deserve you.

There is nothing left. And such an elementary error in the conception three years ago. Was it preventable? That's what I can't for the life of me fathom, but what does it matter, in the end? I'm either a deluded fool or an incompetent.

The storage capacitors buckled under the weight of so much electrical charge. The LGPC worked almost too well, attracting a half-dozen supercell storms in the area, at once. A maelstrom coalescing. My eardrums threatened to rupture. The storms, positive and negative charges, collided. I gazed out at the swirling unnatural scenes unfolding outside the observatory's topmost windows and couldn't believe my eyes. At first. Demonic tendrils of fork lightning and rapid wind shear. Tunnels of air and bolt lightning chased each other like playing children through the sky – so much elemental, destructive power. Slashing, battering, hammering. Updrafts, downdrafts, an avalanche of aural and visual destruction – my human senses unable to process even a fraction of it.

Then a bombardment of explosions. I fell to the floor and tried desperately to save my eardrums. I understood, then, exactly what we mean when we say sound is comprised of sonic vibrations. My nervous system rattled – the intensity was unimaginable – and I find myself, a day later, still shaking as I write this. I can barely hear the thunder now, though I know it is there – only a high-pitched hum.

When the explosions ceased, I collected myself and ran out onto the observatory balcony. Below me, I witnessed devastation. All but three of the lightning rods lay in ruins. Their metal pylons twisted, bent, blackened. The load placed upon them was too much. Simply too much.

Beyond them, beside the small pond where you once played, Adeleine, the storage capacitors had been torn asunder. Fragments lay scattered, askew, some thrown close to fifty metres.

I felt myself scream yet could not hear it. All I felt was the searing pain of my electrical burns, refusing to heal. I collapsed to the ground and didn't move for a very, very long time.

If this is to be my last entry – and it well may be – I want to be remembered as a man who failed, but only in trying. For his family. For you, Adeleine. As ill-conceived an ambition as it may always have been.

I'm not naive. I know I did this for myself more than anyone else. For no other purpose than to restore a world that, maybe, as you often pointed out, Vera, is better left remaining where it is. In the past.

I know we have no real control over how we are remembered and how history is recorded. I may not be remembered at all, which is probably for the best.

17 OCTOBER 2027

The settlement is more or less as I remember it, but at the same time, so much appears changed. Brick shanties with tarpaulins stretched across gaping holes in roofs. The ground is slick with mud and potholed, but this hardly matters in a world with no working cars and few means of transportation.

I think back to that explosion I heard some time ago. Could I have imagined it? Had it been a sign, then, to stop and return to my family? A sign I'd wilfully ignored. Whatever it was, the settlement endured, and here I am. It has been over a week now since my return. Adeleine didn't recognise me at first, but there's time for us to get to know each other all over again.

I assist the requisitions team now. Inventory management, mostly, until I am fit enough to head further out into the world. Maybe. Of a night-time, at the end of a busy day, I sit on the balcony and glance up at the old observatory, our home for so many years. It may only be half a day's walk, but it also feels much further away than that. I don't like to remember it. The years I wasted there, trying to revive a dead world that had brought about this disaster in the first place.

Like I said, I'm not a religious man, but there were things I once believed in. Thunder, for instance. Natural phenomena that reshaped this world, and every one of our lives, with an irrepressible commitment to its own existence and supremacy.

The new world – Adeleine's world – forms around me, day by day. I am fortunate to contribute. To play a role. It's more than I deserve. But I can't help looking up that mountainside, at the domed observatory, and wondering what might have been. Here and now, by my family's side, I must be content with the world as it is, not as it could be.

Yet still I wonder.

ABOUT
THE WRITERS

ABOUT THE WRITERS

This collection of storm writing was created by a range of talented writers and poets.

BEVERLEY LELLO enjoys writing short fiction, poetry and plays. Her short fiction and poetry have won many awards and been published in anthologies, magazines and journals. Her plays have been performed locally and nationally. She has published two collections of short stories, *Tailwind* and *Borrowed Spaces*.

SHALE PRESTON writes in Sydney. She has a PhD in English, and her poetry has been published in a range of literary journals, including *Hermes, Overland, Not Very Quiet, Eucalypt*, and the *Australian Poetry Collaboration*. She is the author of a monograph on Charles Dickens and the co-editor of *Queer Victorian Families: Curious Relations in Literature*.

COLLEEN Z BURKE is a poet and author. Her twelfth poetry collection is *Sculpting a Landscape*. She is also the author of *Doherty's Corner: the Life and Work of Poet Marie E. J. Pitt*, two memoirs, *The Waves Turn* and *The Human Heart is a Bold Traveller*, and is co-editor of the anthology *The Turning Wave: Poems and Songs of Irish Australia*.

JUDE AQUILINA is a writer, editor and teacher of creative writing. Her poems, short stories and articles are published in Australia and abroad. She won the 2018 Barbara Hanrahan Fellowship and has published eight collections of her poetry.

PETER FRANKIS lives and writes on Wodi Wodi land in the industrial town of Port Kembla, south of Sydney. His first poetry chapbook, *Shorely*, was published in 2022 by Ginninderra Press, and his poem *8 ways to look at an octopus* was joint winner of the 2022 Wollongong Art Gallery Prize. He also won the Urban Prize in the Melbourne Union of Poets International Poetry Competition 2023.

SUZI MEZEI lives on lands traditionally owned by the people of the First Nations. She is a Sri Lankan-born writer whose work has appeared in journals and anthologies in Australia and overseas. Her play was performed at La Mama, and she has received writing awards. She is a fan of visual art, films and dogs.

LEONE GABRIELLE writes poetry and prose. She is from Seymour, a snaking river town in central Victoria, Australia, on Taungurung country. She has been published in *Cordite Poetry Review, Australian Poetry Journal, Pure Slush, Plumwood Mountain Journal, Mona Magazine, MASKS Literary Magazine, XR Global,* and *Meanjin Literary Journal.* When not writing, she is in the company of ravens and flowers.

PERRY NARBOROUGH is a young man who finds solace in writing. Working as a biomedical engineer, he relies on writing as an outlet for creative expression. He hopes to one day write a novel.

JIM KENT is a retired Area Postal Manager living in Port Fairy, Victoria. He enjoys writing short stories and bush ballads.

NANDI-LI O'SULLIVAN is seventeen years old. She has always liked reading but recently decided to try her hand at writing. She wants her writing to convey beauty, emotion and introspection.

JADE DICKINSON is thirteen years old and lives in Tasmania, Australia. She loves writing about mythical and spiritual themes and finds it fun to write from the perspective of animals, interpreting their feelings and actions. She believes that everyone and everything should get a chance to tell their story.

MIEKE HEYKOOP started writing stories as soon as she learned to hold a pencil and has been going on vast trips of the imagination since then, taking inspiration from mythology, history, and all things fantastical. While writing is her main passion, she also spends time doodling, playing violin, and learning random facts about history and historical clothing.

BROOKS CARVER is an American writer of historical fiction, a poet, and a photographer. His poems and short stories have appeared in numerous magazines.

NICHOLAS JEFFERS is a Baltimore-based writer hoping to expand his writing career beyond online submissions for contests. He finds writing to be a solution for internal conflict and hopes that his words bestow peace to his readers.

CL GLANZING is an international nomad, currently living in London. By day, she works in healthcare research, trying to use those ridiculous letters after her name (MA, MSc, PhD). By night, she does heritage crafts and runs an LGBTQ+ book club. She has been published in *Luna Station Quarterly*, *The Writing Disorder*, *Jet Fuel Review*, and *The Quarter(ly)*.

MEREDITH DOWNES is a writer of adult and children's fiction, from Brisbane. She has previously been published in *Southerly*. "Battery Life" is a surreal exploration of the impact of weather events, and the loss of light and electricity, on the modern psyche, inspired by Meredith's own experiences living in Queensland, Australia.

CONOR SCANLAN is a writer from Melbourne with a keen interest in all things speculative fiction. He is currently working full-time as a communications officer in the trade union movement while making his first foray into the world of short story writing. You can find out more about his work at https://conorscanlan.com/.

www.ingramcontent.com/pod-product-compliance
Lightning Source LLC
Chambersburg PA
CBHW070330120726
47909CB00008B/2672